THE THREE SPARTANS

Copyright © 2019 James McCann

Library and Archives Canada Cataloguing in Publication

The Three Spartans by James McCann.

McCann, J. Alfred (James Alfred), 1972- author.

ISBN 9781775351542 (softcover)

ISBN 9781775351559 (PDF)

ISBN 9781775351566 (EPUB)

Copy edited by Dawn Loewen

Proofread by Audrey McClellan

Cover design by Rhiannon Davies-Willson

Interior design by Julia Breese

Published by

CRWTH PRESS

#204 – 2320 Woodland Drive

Vancouver, BC V5N 3P2

info@crwth.ca | www.crwth.ca

Printed and bound in Canada.

THE THREE SPARTANS

James McCann

CP | CRWTH PRESS

To my university prof who taught me Thucydides. You instilled in me a love of ancient Greece and the understanding of what it means to read beyond the text.

*Far better is it to have a stout heart always,
and suffer one's share of evils, than to be ever
fearing what may happen.*
—Herodotus, 484–425 BCE

The Histories, Book 7, Chapter 50
(translated by George Rawlinson)

I pressed my body into a corner, clutching my weapon to my chest. Lea was down on the ground, holding off the attack coming at us from the woods. Our army was gone, every soldier either painted or driven far into the woods. If they hadn't been caught already, it was only a matter of time.

Lea's paintball rifle was silent. "Lea! Are you still there?" I shouted through the chaos.

"Still with you, Art!" she shouted back. For the first time this summer I heard defeat in her voice. But me? I wasn't ready to give up. Not yet. Our plan should have worked. We shouldn't be in this mess, under attack from all sides.

Had the Oracle lied to us? No. The unthinkable was true. There had been a traitor in our midst all along.

>>>><<<<

Three days ago, still so innocent, I began my summer the way I always had: at the Fish Shack.

"I don't understand why we have to be here," my dad muttered to my mom. "Art is old enough to meet Lea on his own." The waitress tossed a few menus onto our table and eyed the two empty chairs we were guarding.

"We still need those," Mom said, and the waitress gave us an obviously forced smile. My mom gave a similar fake smile to my dad. It looked a lot like the smile she gave me whenever she asked what I was up to and I started fibbing.

"We're here because the best part of being in Birch Bay is no one here cares what your background is, we all mingle together. Set a good example for your son."

"But the kids will take off right away, and then we're stuck making small talk with—"

"Benny! If it isn't my favourite cottage cowboy." Lea's dad walked onto the patio.

"Anax, how have you been?" My dad stood and shook Anax's hand. Lea stepped around her dad and punched my shoulder.

"How have I been? Benny! I have news of a magnitude that will impress even high rollers such as you."

I looked over at my dad, who looked back at me with pleading eyes. Before anyone else could speak, Anax said, so loudly the whole restaurant could hear, "Let the kids go off on their bikes so the men can speak." Then he laughed and added, "Sorry. The *persons*," nodding at my mom.

My dad gave me another pleading look and my mom gave Lea's dad a forced smile. I shrugged before grabbing my bag of old books and following Lea out.

I looked at the boats stuck in the sand in the low tide. Seagulls picked at fish and shells in shallow pools of water while kids ran in and out of the ocean, laughing. I loved this place. I loved coming here every summer. Hanging out with Lea was a big part of that. We had met two summers earlier at the C Shop, where we were both getting ice cream. I had been holding a Percy Jackson book, and she nodded with approval.

"You like Greek mythology?" she'd asked me. We wound up bonding over a shared love of ancient times. Even though we saw each other only in the summertime, we were still best friends. In Birch Bay, Lea was more popular than me. I was kind of her shadow.

"Sorry about my dad," Lea said as she headed to the bike rack.

"That's okay," I said as I pulled my BMX out of the rack.

"Not sure why he hates summer people so much. No offence."

I never took offence at what her dad said. It was no secret Lea's dad didn't like it when summer visitors came and took over. My mom said it was because he was working while everyone else got to relax. She said we had to be "mindful of our privilege." My mom was a lawyer and my dad wrote video games. Basically, they could be at the cabin the whole summer, since my dad could work from home and my mom could get to Vancouver in a couple of hours.

I pedalled hard to keep up with Lea.

At the C Shop, Lea skidded to a halt, stirring up dust, and I did the same beside her. We looked through the open door at the lineup where families were buying ice cream and fudge. Fishing in my pocket for change, I found a couple of loonies and a Canadian quarter, but they were no use to me in Washington State.

"I'm broke, but I wish I could get some of that amazing fudge."

"Yeah, I'm broke, too," Lea admitted with a sigh. "You want to exchange your books at the bookshop?"

I stared at my coins as if willing them to become US dollars. When they didn't, I said, "Yeah, let's do that."

We walked our bikes down the street to a cabin with bookshelves outside where people could buy or trade used books. There we saw the dreaded red-headed twins, one sitting in a big comfy checkered chair and the other sifting through the books.

"Lookey-lookey," one of them said.

"If it isn't the—"

"—dynamic duo." Whenever one started to speak, the other always finished. They weren't identical; in fact, one was a girl and the other a boy, so telling them apart was easy. But I didn't know their actual names.

"Summer is here, so Art is back!" Lea said and slapped my back. "Anything good here to trade?"

I put my bike down on the grass and walked to the shelf that usually had mythology. Typical stuff—Riordan and the DK encyclopedias.

"You trading—"

"—anything good?" the twins asked, one trying to get a glimpse into my bag. I didn't like chatting too much with them, because they had this ability to get other kids in trouble.

"I got a copy of *Eragon.* It was okay, but I'm in the mood for some Greek history."

"Art's dad helped on a game called *Zero A.D.* about ancient Greece," Lea said. "It's solid. You build armies and fight historical wars."

"What does zero—"

"—A.D. mean?" the twins asked.

"*Zero* is the number zero, and *A.D.* stands for *Anno Domini* in Latin, which means 'year of our Lord,'" I said.

"So *Zero A.D.* was more than two thousand years ago," said Lea.

The twins looked at each other with wide smiles.

I turned back to the shelf and saw a book on Spartans. "Hey, dude, check this out!" I said, showing Lea the cover. When we played *Zero A.D.*, we were always Spartans, these awesome warriors in ancient Greece.

"Can you play—"

"—multiplayer?" the twins asked.

"Yeah. And it's free!" Lea said.

I half listened as she took out her phone and showed them where they could download the game. Taking my books from my bag, I put them on the shelf and traded them for the one on ancient Sparta. My dad was going to love it.

"Thanks for the game tip—"

"—and we got a tip for you."

Lea gave me a look that told me she wasn't in the mood to get into trouble today. "That's okay," I said to the twins and headed for my bike.

"You probably couldn't—"

"—handle it anyway," the twins said with smiles.

"Handle what?" Lea asked. I had forgotten how competitive she could be.

"The new slide—"

"—at the Slide and Glide Water Park. It's got a sixty-foot drop."

"Uhh, I live here." Lea rolled her eyes at them. "I obviously saw them building the Plunge during the winter."

"Sixty feet is nothing," I said. "In Canada, we have a slide that's seventy-two feet at Cultus Lake." The only reason I knew and remembered this was because my aunt took me there. I loved water parks but had been too embarrassed to tell her how much heights scared me. Let's just say they had to close the ride after I got to the top, looked down and lost my lunch. But these guys didn't need to know that.

"You're telling me you got a slide in Canada bigger than us?" This time the voice was from Zeke, my old summertime nemesis. He and I had met two years ago, when he and his dad stopped by our cabin to talk to my parents about selling. Darren Darius Realty bought property and then sold it to developers, and they wanted my parents' cabin. My family had spent every summer here since my dad was my age.

Darren Darius "wins by never saying no," and he didn't take well to my parents asking him to leave. I heard he lost out on some deal because my dad wouldn't sell. Since then, Zeke had always tried to outdo me in front of the other kids. If it was biking, he did the harder trails. Swimming, he joined his school swim team, the Immortals.

Lea looked away from Zeke and I wondered why. She wasn't afraid of anybody.

"By the way," Zeke said in this voice like he was super proud to be the one telling me, "Lea here tell you she's gotta move after this summer?"

"Zeke, why you gotta lie all the time?" I said.

"He's not this time," Lea said with a voice that quivered. "Zeke's dad bought our house. And now we gotta leave."

"Darren Darius Realty makes Birch Bay better." Zeke repeated his dad's slogan and laughed hard. The twins joined him in a chorus of evil cackles.

"But you're staying in Birch Bay, right?" I asked Lea.

"We'll talk about it later," she said.

"Yeah, Art. Why don't you get back to lying about the giant slide you have in Canada?" said Zeke.

"We have a seventy-two-foot slide. It's real," I said, getting angry.

"Even if you did, you're too chicken to do a slide like that," Zeke said.

"Art isn't chicken!" Lea was boiling-over mad. "And he can prove it by doing the Plunge."

"Only one problem," I said quickly. "It costs money to get into that park."

"My brother isn't working today, else I'd get us in," Zeke said.

"We got a few Canadian coins," Lea suggested to the twins.

"Canadian—"

"—coins?"

Yeah. Now it got bad. It was no secret the twins liked Canadian loonies. They were like this guy Charon in Greek mythology who took gold coins in exchange for a ferry ride over to the Underworld. I took out my gold coin and watched as their eyes locked on it. I was actually wishing for the Underworld rather than a sixty-foot slide.

"We can—"

"—get you in," the twins said to the coin.

"Problem solved," Zeke said in a way that made me wonder if he'd heard about the kid losing his lunch at Cultus Lake, put two and two together and realized it was me. There was a video on YouTube, but you couldn't see my face.

"You get us in," Lea said, "and our golden dollar is yours."

"Loonie," I reminded Lea, and she laughed.

"Follow us," the twins said in unison.

As we followed them, I tried to come up with some believable excuse to get out of there. I couldn't say "I don't have my swim trunks" because I was wearing them, hoping to go to the beach later. We cut through a few businesses and took the side streets to get to the water park. Standing at the back of the parking lot, I swallowed hard. On either side of the gates, a red-brick building spanned the length of the large parking lot. Chain-link fence encircled the rest of the grounds, and behind were Douglas firs that made the park look as if it were in the middle of the wilderness. I could see the slide tops from behind the building. And on the far right, the Plunge rose as high as the trees themselves.

My stomach clenched. We locked up our bikes at the rack and followed the twins and

Zeke to the back of the water park. The twins knocked on a door with no sign on it, four quick, a pause, and then two quick.

"Morse code—"

"—for *hi*."

The door opened and there was a kid there, looking around and waving us in. The twins went first, then Zeke, then Lea. She turned to me when I didn't follow and gave me her raised eyebrows. What was I going to say at that point? That I was afraid of puking at the top of the slide?

I was stuck. This was happening.

I followed them inside through a series of back-way corridors that led to the slides. "Listen," Lea said as we walked into the open area where the crowd of kids was splashing in the pools or chatting in the lines to the slides.

Screaming. So much screaming reached our ears. I looked up, way up, and saw the sixty-foot slide known as the Plunge. My mom would have used her dictionary words like *magnificent* or *resplendent*. But no word could fully capture its glory. My legs started to shake and my breakfast started to stir in my stomach. It was as though I had been transported back to when I had stood atop the seventy-two-foot slide in Cultus Lake.

Okay, big shot," Zeke said. "Let's see you take the Plunge."

"You crazy?" I said. That got his attention. He paused for a second to let me continue. "This your first time at a water park?"

This was my one shot to get out of this.

"I love corn dogs—no way I'm going on a waterslide on an empty stomach."

"What?" Zeke looked at the twins. I'm pretty sure it was working.

"Yeah. The way they deep-fry the bread right onto the hot dog, and then you eat it from a stick. Pure. Genius."

I wasn't sure what the next move was. Pretend to choke? Say I was too full? Maybe I'd get lucky and the water park would catch on fire. Fire was unlikely, sure, but I was desperate.

"You know, one guy, a few years back—"

"—ate before going down a slide and drowned," the twins said. I was pretty sure that never happened, even if it seemed like the sort of story that would be true.

"Yeah, I heard that," Lea said, her cheeks turning a shade of crimson that told me she had never heard that. I really didn't want her to see me pass out or puke at the top of the Plunge. "Besides, we have no money."

"No more excuses," Zeke said and walked over so he was chest to chest with me. "Either you admit you're too chicken to do that slide, or you go do it."

Then George ran up to us. "Art! You're here! Hey, Lea, what's going on?" His voice had this sudden switch to soprano in mid-sentence.

"Art's going to do the Plunge."

"Geez, did you hear about the kid on the slide in Canada that threw up at the top? You gotta check out the YouTube—"

"I'm doing it!" I said as Zeke and the twins took out their phones. The day had started out with so much promise.

I walked to the first set of stairs and looked up at the six flights. I gave a nod to Lea, who stood with her arms crossed as if proud we were about to show up Zeke.

Other kids gathered as Zeke pointed at me. Although I couldn't hear him anymore, I could see his mouth make the words "Canada" and "bigger slide" and then, looking directly at me, "chicken."

There was no way I was spending my summer as the kid who lost to Zeke. I watched as others walked up the six flights of stairs and took the Plunge. I walked the first flight, then the second flight, and I suddenly lost my balance. As I grabbed the metal bar, I started to feel dizzy. The ground was so far down now. A bunch of kids scooted past me. Younger kids too, which made it worse.

Breathing deeply, I moved one foot after the next. I managed the third set of stairs and then the fourth.

"Hey, you don't have to do this," Lea said as she rushed up behind me. I could hear Zeke's jeers as he got all the kids to make clucking noises.

"I do, Lea. No way am I letting Zeke win."

She walked with me on the fifth set of stairs. When we emerged at the top, my heart was beating so hard that my chest hurt.

"Did you really do the slide in that lake?" she asked.

"Cultus Lake, and it's a water park." I didn't want to lie to Lea. "Not exactly. I kind of—"

"HA!" Zeke shouted from below. "HE PUKED!"

Below us, Zeke was showing a group of kids something on his phone. In turn, kids were running to their lockers and taking out their phones and showing them off. George climbed up to join us.

"Aww, man. I'm so sorry. I didn't know that was you," he said.

"What?" Lea scrunched her face and took out her phone. She looked on as George pulled up what I assumed was the video of me puking. My stomach wrenched and I had to hold back the breakfast that was still digesting.

"There's one that was taken by some guy who was standing behind you in line," George said.

My face burned and I felt like I couldn't breathe. I'll be honest, I wanted to cry. I didn't care that everyone else knew, but I never wanted Lea to think of me as the loser who puked at Cultus Lake. The laughter from the kids made me want to disappear, and I ran down all the stairs. Lea shouted after me, but that just made me go faster. I ran, pushing my way through the crowd. Once I was through the gate, I grabbed my bike and pedalled home.

I wanted to play video games and watch TV that afternoon—anything that involved lying around on the couch. But this was "the cabin," so we had no TV. And I'd used up my hour of laptop time for the day. So that only left lying around doing nothing. I didn't have a phone, so at least Lea couldn't text me.

"Lea called again," my mom told me, holding her cell phone out in a way that suggested I should call Lea back.

"Yeah, thanks," I said as I grabbed a magazine from the coffee table and pretended to read.

"You feeling bad that Lea's moving to Seattle?"

Lea's moving to Seattle? That's why she hadn't wanted to talk about it before. This summer hit a whole new level of sucking. "Mom, seriously, I'm busy right now."

"Really? How's that copy of *Cabin Life* working out for you?"

I looked at what I was reading and dug in. "Fine, Mom. Fine. When we want to replace the roof, you'll be glad I read it."

"Come to the table. Your dad is sitting in front of his Game Master screen waiting to play. It's sad to see him at the table all alone." Then she said under her breath, loud enough for me to hear, "But not as sad as you look."

Basilisks & Ballistae is a storytelling game where one person, usually my dad, plays the author of the tale and everyone else acts out characters. It's like one of those Choose Your Own Adventure books, but you make the story choices with dice and special rules.

I pulled myself off the couch and walked to the game. A gridded map that had trees and grass painted on it to make it look like the woods was spread out on the table. Through the trees, a brown dirt path was drawn. In the middle of the woods was a plastic knight with a shield and sword. In front of my chair were six dice, all with different numbers of sides: four, six, eight, ten, twelve and twenty.

"Ahhh! The hoplite warrior returns to the field of battle!" my dad said. He'd made up what he called a "homebrew" version of *Basilisks & Ballistae* based on ancient Greece. Hoplites were Greek soldiers.

"You are facing an armed orc warrior." My dad's voice became very grave as he handed me a twenty-sided dice and the paper with all my character information.

"I attack with my sword." I half-heartedly gave the dice my famous "wrist-twist." It bounced around on the table until it finally showed us a twelve.

I almost missed Lea's signature knock, this corny "shave-and-a-haircut" pattern I had never even heard of until I met her. Mom traitorously let Lea in.

"Did you hit?" Lea asked as she pulled up a chair.

My dad answered in the British accent he gave every knight he played and babbled something about a flesh wound. He and my mom started giggling.

My dad handed Lea a character sheet. Since my dad pretty much always had a *Basilisks & Ballistae* game running, Lea had played with us a few times every summer.

"You are, once again, a hoplite paladin, Lea. A Spartan warrior always wanting to do the right thing."

Lea took it and looked it over. "Was this a real thing?"

"Not exactly. The hoplites were real soldiers in Sparta, but I took the paladin idea from the original rules of B&B."

Lea nodded, but Dad didn't notice. He was busy looking at his screen.

"Okay!" he said. "You see a barbarian in the distance running toward you. You may each take one more move before this stranger is upon you."

"I prepare a fireball spell. Whoever moves next gets it," said my mom. She had loved playing wizards ever since she read Harry Potter. Before that, she was strictly a rogue, or so my dad liked to tell me. Apparently, they met at a role-playing-game convention.

Lea started picking up random dice and dropping them on the table for no reason.

Every time the dice hit the wood, the sound jabbed at my ears. I didn't understand why Lea was even here after what had happened today. I didn't know what to say, and our game was crashing to a halt.

A look passed between my mom and dad before my mom said, "I think we could use popcorn."

"That would be great!" my dad said, but then my mom smirked at him and he stood. "Oh! Right. How about I help you get it?"

When my parents were in the kitchen, Lea reached into her knapsack and took out a wooden board the size of a house shingle.

"I made you this," Lea mumbled as she put it on the table. "I don't care that you puked on some stupid slide."

Now I was picking up random dice and tossing them on the table. "Thanks. Sorry I freaked out. Everyone laughing at me was just so embarrassing."

"You should've stuck around. Zeke got one of the lifeguards to kick me out for not paying to get in. That was embarrassing, too."

"What? Zeke didn't pay either."

"Like that matters!" she said.

"He acts like he owns Birch Bay, just because his dad is some big shot realtor."

"Hey," I said. "Sucks you have to move to Seattle."

"Yeah," said Lea. "But at least we have the rest of the summer."

And just like that, we were friends again. It was what I liked about Lea, we never had grudges, no matter the disagreement. My dad returned with two bowls and handed us the one with butter. His had some sort of spice that was "good for the heart, but still edible."

My dad picked up the sign, his eyes growing super wide, and held it with both hands outstretched.

"SPARTA!" he yelled. "Hey, did you kids see my latest mod for *Zero A.D.*?"

Lea punched my shoulder hard. It kind of hurt. "No! Art never said you made another mod. Solid! But I thought you work for some big company now."

"I do, but I do love me some ancient times. *Zero A.D.* is a—"

"—labour of love," my mom said as she returned with kale chips, her version of popcorn. To me they tasted like cyanide. Not that I've ever had cyanide, but I'm sure it would taste like kale.

"Did you want to stay for dinner, Lea?" my mom asked.

Dinner at my house was always an experience because my mom was vegetarian and my dad and I ate meat. Most times I recognized the things on my plate, unless it was my mom's turn to cook and she made one of her casserole dishes. She didn't put meat into those, though sometimes she put in stuff that looked like it could be meat.

We had Lea's dad over for dinner once. Lea and I had wanted to have a sleepover, and so it was an audition to see if my parents felt comfortable with me staying over at Lea's. I'm pretty sure what got them was when Lea's dad took a mouthful of the mock-meat casserole and said, "If meat tasted this awful, we'd all be vegetarian."

My dad suggested we have the sleepover at our house. Lea's dad had said, "Get rid of this kid for a night? Take 'er."

Every summer Lea ate over here so often she didn't even call home. I didn't know what she did the rest of the year.

"If I stay, could Art and I play the new mod?"

Lea was brilliant. If I'd asked, my mom would have said no because I got one hour on my laptop a day and she had to stay consistent. I'd heard her speech so often I had it memorized. But Lea asking meant my mom had to consider it. My mom knew Lea and I loved this game and my dad would want to show off his new modification.

My mom gave my dad a look. This was going to be tricky. They often had these annoying conversations without speaking to each other. They said it happened when you knew someone as well as they knew each other.

"It's our first day back; I'm good with the kids playing on the laptop for a while. I can play my guitar and you can read your book."

I could tell by my mom's face that my dad had gotten the message wrong. But I jumped on my dad's offer.

"Just until dinner's made. So Lea can see Dad's mod."

My mom looked at her watch and said, "Twenty more minutes. That's it. Dinner is a few hours away, and you're not playing for that long."

"Even that's good," I said. "Thanks, Mom!" Lea nodded and echoed my thanks.

I started collecting character sheets and dice. I didn't notice my dad was already in his den until the screech of an electric guitar suddenly shook the house. My dad often played his guitar while blasting music from the '80s and '90s he had learned when he was in a cover band. We had a bunch of photos around the cottage of a teenager with long frizzed-out black hair and eyeliner—my dad the rock star.

The music had a couple of big beats and then a pause. He was singing Queen's "We Will Rock You."

"Man, sometimes I wish he could be a normal dad."

"Like mine?" Lea's words instantly reminded me I had no reason to complain—ever. For a moment we listened to my dad's music.

Lea sang along with my dad, holding out her fist to me. I laughed as we fist-bumped, and it was like the playlist had healed what may have been left of our rift.

"What was your dad's band called again?" Lea asked, walking over to the couch and sinking into a cushion.

"The Oracle. Named after mystical fortune tellers in ancient Greece who offered people advice from the gods."

"I know what an oracle is," Lea said. She mouthed the words to the song my dad was playing.

I sat on the couch beside Lea. When I opened my laptop, the game was already running so I proudly showed her my Spartan village. It was bustling with an agora, the main place where people gathered for public announcements; a few farms; storage buildings; and a port with many, many ships.

"Your navy is impressive. You like building ships, huh?" She took out her laptop and loaded up *Zero A.D.* so she could also play. Her ancient laptop was slow, but the game still ran on it. Lea and I have an alliance in the game, and we normally play against the computer on a private server.

"Yeah." My navy was good, but she was impressive at gathering troops. Lea was a master at the game.

I noticed two other kids had joined, Malcolm and Courtney. I gave Lea a shrug to see if she knew how they got onto our server.

"I gave the twins the info today, remember? They have actual names, doofus."

But there was another kid playing on our server. Playing as the Persians, and he was aligned with the twins—and building a big army.

"They gave the info to Zeke? Really?" I said.

"Kick him off," Lea said and started moving my mouse.

"No!" I was all smiles at this point. Zeke may have been important in Birch Bay, but he was in our world now. He dared to come into the land of ancient Greece where Lea and I reigned supreme. "We can totally beat him. No way are his Persians going to beat our Spartans."

"He must have been playing since we left the water park," Lea said. "If he set his speed to insane, he might have built up an army that could compete with us."

I sighed with impatience.

"We can beat him," Lea said quickly. "I'm just saying we need to be smart about it. The twins are on his side."

"Plus, I'll start my dad's mod." I clicked a menu button that brought up a screen of game options. As the server owner, I could control what game modes *Zero A.D.* had running. I chose "Battle of the 300," and the landscape changed between where Zeke's Persians had their camp and where our cities were built. "The only way Zeke's Persians can get to Sparta is through the Thermopylae Pass, this narrow pathway through the mountains. Even if he gets a huge army together, there's no way they can attack all at once."

Lea nodded. "All our previous armies and cities stay the same? Your dad's mod didn't change that?"

I shook my head. "It only changes the map. Everything else stays the same."

"You gather your ships and sail them here"— she read the map—"to Thermopylae. I'll take my troops and march them to bottleneck the pass."

"I'll defend the water; you defend the ground."

Then we saw Zeke's army, with Malcolm and Courtney's, marching through the pass. Ships also sailed by sea; I sent my ships to take them out. Lea commanded her troops to stand firm and fight only when attacked.

A chat box opened, and Zeke said: *Surprised the water doesn't make all your ships puke.*

I wrote back: *Your ships will be puking when I'm done with them.*

"Good one," Lea said and laughed.

Sure enough, Zeke's army had to march in small numbers to get through the pass. As my ships met with Zeke's, and Lea's soldiers met with Malcolm and Courtney's, the battle at Thermopylae began.

"Okay, your twenty minutes is up," my mom called from the porch.

If we quit now, Zeke would win by default. "Hold on, Mom! Five more minutes!"

And then the worst thing happened, a life-is-over kind of moment. The internet went dead, and our connection dropped. All that was left of the game was a big box telling us we lost the battle. Both Lea and I held up our arms and shouted, "Noooo!"

My mom appeared in the room, rolling her eyes the way she did when she thought I was being overly dramatic. But we were being under-dramatic considering what she'd done. "Mom, you basically made us lose to our arch-enemy."

"Plus," Lea said with eyes wide, "Zeke thinks we quit. He thinks we gave up."

"Go outside and play," my mom said. "You've got the beach, a forest and one of the most beautiful estuaries in Washington to enjoy this summer. You can play that game any time you want."

"Mom! You don't understand!"

"I was twelve once, and we didn't spend all our time on our computers. And yes, we did have computers!" Mom gave me a glare that challenged me to make an "old person" joke, like computers weren't invented yet so that's why she didn't spend all her time on one. I knew better at this point, so I kept my mouth shut.

"Go to the water park or the beach, or play paintball! We got you that gear last summer, and it's hardly been used."

I gave her a loud sigh to tell her none of that interested me right now.

"What about the treehouse?" My mom was now shooing us toward the door as she said this.

"Right. Because we're still six."

"You played there last year." Mom gave us another eye roll.

"We are not going to the treehouse!" That last part I yelled from outside after my mom closed the door on us. Lea shrugged as she got on her bike, so I did the same and we rode down the lane.

"Where do you want to go?" Lea asked.

"Might as well go to the treehouse. Nothing else to do."

As much as I didn't want to go to the treehouse, it was in the opposite direction from the water park. Plus, it was the least likely place we'd run into Zeke or anyone else. Was this going to be a long summer of hiding from everyone?

We rode our bikes down the road past Beachwood Grocery and Deli, through the campsites to the trail that led to the treehouse. We left our bikes at the mouth of the trail.

We walked a winding dirt path through giant black cottonwood trees that rose straight up, farther than you could see, and paper birch that had bark you could actually use to write messages on. The path wound its way to a treehouse that had been here since my dad was my age.

I didn't want to admit it, but the treehouse was one of my favourite things in Birch Bay. It wasn't actually in a tree, but it looked like it was suspended in the air by a Douglas fir that grew right beside it. It had a ladder that went into a hole in the bottom. On all sides, open windows allowed you to see nature.

The front of the treehouse faced the path, but the back overlooked the woods. The campsites were just far enough away that no noise reached us. The calls of chickadees and squirrels were our soundtrack. I climbed up the ladder, feeling like this was a pretty good place to spend my summer of shame. Cloth drapes covered the windows, so I tied them open to look out.

Lea followed me inside and leaned on the windowsill facing the back. "Hey, an eagle."

I went over to check it out. Eagles were common birds of prey here on the Pacific West Coast, but I thought they were the coolest birds ever. I saw one in a bird refuge once, and it was nearly as big as me. Also, they made the weirdest sound for a bird of prey. Almost like some sort of comic-book villain's cackle. I looked through the other windows at the surrounding stinging nettles, most at least a few feet high. Stinging nettles had tiny hairs, and if you touched them, they caused an itchy rash that could ruin an otherwise great week. I walked through a bunch last year and was done for three days.

Lea took out her phone. "We need music," she said and started tapping the screen. "Did you know your dad has a playlist on Spotify called *The Oracle*? It's all the covers his band used to play."

"You follow my dad on Spotify?"

"I just found him now," she said in a *duh* kind of tone. "Also, I found your dad's band on Vimeo. Check it out."

She showed me the video, like I hadn't been forced to watch it a thousand times. Lea turned up the volume and we listened to the guitar and drums play loud and fast. "Your dad is good," Lea said with a nod of respect.

"Don't tell him that. He'll wind up putting the band back together again."

When the vocals came on, Lea sang along with my teenage dad. She started dancing around as she belted out this song about standing up for who you are and what you believe.

"I think the Oracle's playlist is speaking to us!" said Lea, now dancing around me and waving her arms as if for me to join her.

I scrunched my face. "It's a band called Accept. I seriously doubt that."

Lea pushed between me and the window to get my attention.

"How can you not get this? This song is all about living for something and trusting ourselves and standing up for that." Lea waited, as if expecting me to understand where she was going with this. When I didn't, she continued with even more passion. "Yeah, you got embarrassed because you puked on some Canadian slide and someone put it on YouTube. But is that going to ruin our entire summer? Or do we use it to make this the best summer ever?"

I gave her a sidelong glance that kept my vision on the eagle while also taking note of her mental breakdown. Puke was not going to make this the best summer ever.

But as the next song played, the lyrics started taking hold of me. Bryan Adams, a fellow Canadian, seemed to be telling me that this summer *would* be the best ever. I understood that, like the oracles in ancient Greece, my dad's playlist of old music *was* speaking to us.

"So what do we do—?"

She threw me a grimace that told me she was still working out the details. "I have an idea. You think your parents would let you camp here without them for a few days?"

"Not in a million years."

"If we can camp here, we can challenge Zeke to a game of paintball. Winner takes the water park."

"Interesting," I said with a raise of my eyebrows.

"If we get the water park back, we take away Zeke's power."

"And show Zeke he isn't a despot," I added with emphasis.

"Despot?" Lea asked. "Is that one of your mom's words?"

I nodded.

"Look at the path. Zeke won't be able to send more than three at a time," said Lea. "The nettles and poison oak make going through the woods way harder."

"Like my dad's mod of that battle in ancient Sparta!" I said.

"You in?" she asked, but she already knew I was in. This was the last summer I'd have with Lea, and the only chance we had to beat Zeke together. This would mean the guy who puked in Cultus Lake would be known as the guy who put Zeke in his place!

We rode all over Birch Bay looking for Zeke. He wasn't at the C Shop (but that amazing fudge was, and this time I had a few bucks) or outside the water park or even at the library. Just when we started thinking he might have gone home, I had an idea. "The private beach." I pointed toward it, and Lea nodded. "Can't believe we didn't start there."

We rode the path along the bay until we got to a gated area. On the other side was a short bridge and a beach where a family was splashing in the water beside a docked rowboat. Zeke was in the water with a few kids from the Immortals swim team, and it looked like he was instructing them in a swim move.

"That's called 'the fly,' and it's some kind of hard swim move," Lea said to me. "Zeke's been bragging that he mastered it."

"Bet you can't do it," we said in unison in mock-Zeke voices.

I put my bike away at a rack, as did Lea. I unlocked the gate, and we walked the bridge to the island. I knew the code because my dad had paid the fee for us to use it.

"She's not allowed in here," Zeke said and pointed at Lea.

"She is if she's with me." I hoped I sounded more confident than my churning stomach felt. Zeke had a way of making me feel unimportant.

"I have a proposition for you," I said loudly so everyone could hear. I wanted this speech to be epic, like what a Spartan king would have given to his enemies to make them fear his power. It sucked that my voice cracked at that moment.

"What's that, pukinator? Or do you prefer pukester?"

I ignored the laughs.

"You know the old treehouse?" I could tell by their faces they didn't. "There's a treehouse deep in the woods past all the campsites. We challenge you to a game of paintball—at the treehouse. You have to take that treehouse from us by the end of the weekend. Winner takes the water park—and this beach!"

Lea gave me a look as if to say "Nice!"

Zeke's eyes widened for a split second, and that showed me he wasn't certain of victory. It made me feel braver.

"Birch Bay Rollback Weekend starts tomorrow," he said. Rollback Weekend was a car show that took over all of Birch Bay.

"You're twelve. You have some classic car you plan on driving?" Lea said in her most mocking tone.

"Here are the rules," I said. "When someone gets hit, they walk off and never return. Splatter doesn't count. The hit must be dead on. Everyone must wear a helmet. Plus, everyone must use eco-friendly paintballs."

"What if someone who's not in the game wanders by? Like a grown-up?" one of the Immortals asked.

"Grown-ups mean immediate ceasefire," Lea said.

"Why do you get to start with the treehouse?" asked another kid.

I hadn't thought of that. Our plan wouldn't work if we were the attackers.

"You can start in the treehouse if you want," Lea said. What was she doing? We were going to lose before we started.

That wasn't the plan!

Zeke turned to his swim team and they huddled. It took forever, but when they came from their huddle they were smiling.

"We'll do it," Zeke agreed. "We meet at Helweg and Jackson Road at eight."

"Do you want to start in the treehouse?" I asked.

"And get stuck waiting around for you losers to come up with a strategy? No way," said Zeke. "Besides, it will be more fun taking the treehouse from you."

I tried to hide my relief at Zeke's answer. I walked up to him and held out my fist. He slammed his fist down on mine, and Lea and Zeke did the same thing. This was what my dad referred to as a "gentleman's agreement."

"We got work to do," I said to Lea.

Getting Zeke to agree to this wasn't the most difficult challenge for us. That would be getting my parents to agree to it. How were we going to convince my parents to let me camp without adults?

III

The first thing we did was check out my garage for supplies. We had an old Coleman cooler, a tent, a camp stove and three sleeping bags.

"We only need two, but could we take the third in case we get cold?" Lea asked.

I nodded, looking around for anything else we might use. We had a tarp my aunt used for her car when she visited, but the sunny blue sky made me think we didn't need it. I found some rope and put it with the camping supplies.

I found my box of paintball gear. There were enough paintballs to last the weekend and two paintball rifles, one for me and one for Lea.

When I saw my helmet, this wave of glee filled me. It was a typical paintball helmet, but my dad had adorned it with a crest made of feathers on top like a helmet the ancient Spartans wore.

"You have two of those?" Lea asked.

That was the thing with my dad—when he learned Lea loved ancient Greece as much as we did, he started to include her in all his ancient Greece schemes. He'd made four of these helmets so I could invite Lea paintballing this summer. I kind of wished I could bring my mom on our team; she was an amazing sharpshooter.

"I do." I showed her the helmet. Muffled songs from the Oracle filled the space around us, something by Bon Jovi about not being born to follow. When I peeked out of the garage, I saw my mom in her hammock on the porch, deep in a Stephen King novel.

"All we need is to pack that cooler with food and ice for three days," Lea said.

The music stopped, and Dad shouted out the door that dinner was being served in fifteen minutes.

"Thanks, Dad!" I shouted.

"And you kids are up to—?" my dad said as he came into the garage.

Too soon! Lea and I hadn't had time to figure out what we would say. This was where having a dad who couldn't care less was a bonus. Lea could get dressed in full Spartan gear and yell goodbye, and her dad wouldn't even look away from the TV. But my dad was an "involved" parent.

"We're going to play paintball in the woods with some friends. We'll camp after." I said this as matter-of-factly as possible, like this was a thing I did all the time.

"Hmm. No parents? I could come."

I rolled my eyes. "You're being too City. It's not like I'm camping in Stanley Park." My dad would assume we would go to the campground that was a five-minute bike ride away. It felt less like a lie if I didn't say the whole truth.

"You know it's the Rollback Weekend, right?"

"Uh, yeah! That's why we want to be in the woods the next few days."

My dad pursed his lips. "Aunt Sam will be in town. She'll want to see you."

"I can still see her." I could figure out what to do when, and if, that happened. Aunt Sam didn't always show up to things when she said she would.

"Mmmm, I'll talk it over with your mom. You need paintballs?" my dad asked. "We have extras in the van."

"Thanks," I said. My dad's kindness made it harder to lie to him, but we needed to do this — not only for us but for all the kids that Zeke had ever ruled over.

"Come inside, eat dinner and then maybe you can go hang out with your friends."

"Let me get this right," my mom said. "You want to camp in the *campground*" — she stressed that last word and I cringed a little — "play paint-ball in the *woods* and do this on *your own*."

"You're being too City," my dad said as he winked at me. "They'll be five minutes away."

My mom stared at my dad, and I knew they were deep in secret conversation. Judging by my dad's red face, the message had gotten through this time. She turned on me.

"You used that on him? Well, it won't work on me."

"Mrs. Demus," Lea said in her sad voice. She even used a formal greeting instead of my mom's first name. "This is my last summer in Birch Bay. I just want Art and me to have one last adventure."

My mom paused. I looked at her, then my dad and lastly at Lea. This was iffy. But if anyone could convince my mom this was okay, Lea was the one for the job.

"You'll use eco-friendly paint?"

I nodded. I didn't dare risk using words, in case I completely undid whatever magic Lea had cast.

"Does Lea have her phone?" my mom asked.

Lea nodded. She, like me, knew better than to say too much.

"We'll keep ours on in case you need us," my mom said. "We are five minutes away, and there is a park ranger."

"We can do it?" I asked to confirm. It's always good to get confirmation when a message may be unclear.

"Yes. Yes, you can," said Mom.

"Thanks!" Both Lea and I hugged her.

We scarfed down our meal so we could get on the road. My dad let us take some cans of ravioli and SpaghettiOs, plus we remembered a can opener. We also took a loaf of bread, peanut butter, some hot dogs from the freezer and two big jugs of ice for the cooler.

It took us two trips to get everything set up. On our first trip, we had to find a campsite. Rollback Weekend was making that hard.

"Maybe this is why your parents agreed. They knew a spot wouldn't be open," Lea said.

I tapped my foot. Was this how things would end? Was this it?

"Wait," I said as I saw an available spot. The trees hung overhead blocking out the sunlight, leaving it dark and cold. The uneven ground was filled with rocks, which was probably why no one had taken it. It was perfect for us.

We dropped our gear in the site and headed back to the house to say goodbye.

"You two all set? We'll come check on you tomorrow and see how you're doing."

"You don't have to do that, Mom. Really." I tried not to sound desperate.

"Yes, we do," my dad said sternly. Lea nudged me in the ribs, and I took that as a hint to stop before causing suspicion. We could figure out what to do tomorrow.

Before we left, Lea opened her laptop. She still had *Zero A.D.* running. The internet was back on, so she was connected to the server.

"There's a ton of other kids logged in," Lea said. "Zeke must have really spread the word."

I pushed her aside and turned on the chat box.

Calling all Zero A.D. *players*, I typed.

There's a real war brewing. We need soldiers. Grab your paintball gear and meet us at the corner of Helweg and Jackson Road at eight tonight. There's a treehouse deep in the woods past the main campsites. We'll be defending it against Zeke and his Immortals. If he wins, he gets to continue his reign over the water park. If we win, he can't go near the water park all summer. We need you!

"Solid." Lea nodded her approval and shut her laptop. I ran and put it away in my room, and we grabbed the last of our gear. It was time to do this.

⋙⋗⋘

We had to make it look like we were camping at the grounds and not deep in the woods, holding a fort with paintball gear. I hated lying to my parents, but the importance of what we were doing was too great to ignore.

"How do we do this?" Lea asked as we slowed our bikes at the campsite.

"We set up our tent here and pretend to be camping."

"Are you the kids who are going against Zeke?" a young girl asked as she ran up.

I wondered if this was some sort of trap.

"How do you know about Zeke?" Lea asked with the exact level of mistrust I felt.

The girl looked back at her parents who were cooking up dinner.

"I went to the water park today, and he wouldn't let me on the slide I wanted to go on. He said his brother would throw me out if I said anything. A couple other kids told me about you, and I want you to win."

I had an idea. She wanted us to win, so she might help. "My parents may come looking for us." I said. "Can you text us if they do?"

"I'll tell them you went to the bathroom and send you a text."

"Perfect!" said Lea. She gave the girl her number.

We stashed our stuff, raised a tent and made it look like we were camping there.

"It's going to be tricky to get here tomorrow."

"Actually, I have an idea," I said. "Grown-ups mean ceasefire, so all I have to do is get my mom or dad to meet us near the treehouse."

"Nice!" Lea said.

I took a deep breath. "There's no taking this back."

"We can do this, Art. Even if no one else shows, you and I can beat them."

She held out her fist, and I slammed mine down on hers.

→>>>>✖<<<<←

After stashing some gear at the treehouse, we headed to the corner of Helweg and Jackson. No longer were we the innocent children we had been earlier that day. We walked our bikes up to where Zeke and his pack waited. He had at least a dozen other kids on his side. I hoped someone from *Zero A.D.* would show.

"You came," Zeke said. "I thought you would have chickened out like you did at the top of the Plunge."

Lea looked like she might slug him. That would have ended our competition right there, and probably even got me grounded, so I quickly acted.

"Immortals, you may feel an allegiance to Zeke, but are you happy with him always in charge? And you may think you're on the winning side, but you are not. Zeke is going down. Do you want to go down with him? Side with me and Lea, and you will be free to swim or slide all summer long, and you will be my personal guests on the private beach."

"Nice," Lea whispered to me.

Zeke looked at his crew as if waiting for them to switch sides. They didn't.

"I guess we better get set up and ready," Lea said.

"Yeah. You got five minutes, and then it's game on," Zeke said.

IV

It took five minutes at least to get to the treehouse, and while we still had sunlight, I climbed the ladder to get a good look around. A cold breeze rose as crickets chirped. We hid the ladder and tied the rope we'd brought with us as the way in and out of the treehouse. That way, if we got overrun, it would be harder for our enemy to get to us.

It was starting to get dark. "Even if we only last the night," Lea said, "you won't be remembered as the kid who puked anymore."

"What are the chances Zeke will attack tonight?" I asked, dodging the puke comment.

Lea rolled her sleeping bag out on the floor

and then opened the drapes on the front window. She squinted outside.

"They'll need flashlights. We'd have something to aim at. We'd tag them out in a matter of seconds."

"Bet he comes in the morning, full-on assault, and tries to take the treehouse quickly." I rolled out my sleeping bag beside Lea's.

"Should we take watches? One hour on, one hour off?"

I nodded. I scrounged in my pack until I found the sign Lea had carved. By the way she smiled when I held it out, she'd had no idea I'd brought it. I shouted "SPARTA!" like my dad had, and Lea shouted with me.

Later, as I lay down to sleep, I thought about the coming battle. I had never seen a kid who was a better shot than Lea. I'm good, too, but nowhere near Lea's league. This was a war we could win, even if no one who saw our plea on *Zero A.D.* showed. That night I dreamed of victory.

We were up by sunrise and too nervous for breakfast. We put the picnic table on its side as a barrier and Lea huddled behind it. She could see and poke her muzzle through the slats in the boards. I stayed in the treehouse where I could see the woods and listen for changes in bird calls or the rustle of trees. To be honest, I had a feeling Zeke would want us to know when he was coming. I doubted he'd be stealthy.

What never occurred to us was that he might not come at the first crack of light. As the day wore on toward noon, we got restless. Boredom settled in. We broke open tins of ravioli and popped the tops of cans of cola. Our weapons lay relaxed at our sides. I even had my feet propped up against the wall.

Perhaps this had been Zeke's plan all along, I realized, when the first paintball zinged past my chest, exploding on the wall beside me. I scrambled too quickly and knocked my weapon out of the treehouse. I watched it fall as if in slow motion, hitting the ground and bouncing past the cover of the picnic table. Lea hadn't noticed as she scanned the woods with her scope.

I stayed crouched on my stomach, mentally

listing ways I could retrieve the paintball rifle without getting hit. I couldn't take the chance that Zeke had missed on purpose and was toying with me. Every thought started with me leaving the treehouse and instantly getting taken out.

Lea took three shots. They were slow and methodical, so I knew she could see what she was shooting. If she could keep them at bay, perhaps I could scale down the Douglas fir and join her below. We'd lose our advantage of a bird's-eye view, but without a weapon what advantage was that anyway?

The other, far more dangerous possibility was climbing out the back window. The stinging nettles and poison oak behind the treehouse made it nearly impossible to flank us. I would be a visible target, but not an easy one. I imagined myself swinging down the tree with the rope, hitting the dirt and rolling over the grass. I'd scoop up the paintball gun, fire a few rounds and leap behind the picnic table. Maybe if I could imagine it, I could do it.

The Immortals fired more rounds from the woods. Instead of smoking out Lea, they were firing directly at the fort. I had no cover, and if

I tried to climb out, they'd quickly shoot me. I had hesitated too long. I was stuck. We were going to get painted.

"Time to give up," Lea said, her voice flat. I knew she was right. She started to put down her weapon, but paintballs were still flying.

"Wait!" I shouted. Not all the paintballs were shooting *at* us. Some were shooting *into* the woods! Someone had come to help, but who?

A kid emerged from the woods wearing a helmet that hid his face. He ran past my paint-ball rifle, scooped it up and tossed it to me. Then he joined Lea, and together they fired into the woods. I joined the fight. Soon, no more rounds were returned, and the danger had passed. How long that might last we had no way of knowing.

"Thanks for the help," I shouted down to the kid who had thrown me my weapon. "How did you know we were at war?"

"You called it out on *Zero A.D.* I wasn't gonna come, but then I heard Zeke bragging about it at the general store yesterday. They bought out the last of the marshmallows for their victory party, so I bought out the last of the paintball supplies."

The kid took off his helmet, and it was George.

"Dude! You're now one of us, the Spartans!" I said.

"Spartans?" George looked from me to Lea.

"Yeah, like the ancient Greek warriors," Lea said.

"Like the game? That's solid!" George said.

I climbed down to the forest floor and punched his shoulder. And that's when I understood how selfish Lea and I were. We had ruined his whole weekend.

"You can't go home for the whole Birch Bay Rollback Weekend," I told him. "Zeke will have posts along the path, cutting us off from town."

"By now he'll have recruited anyone hoping to go to the water park," said Lea.

"I'm sticking this out," George said. He sounded like my dad when he was mad at me.

I nodded, and as if reading my mind, Lea opened the cooler and checked on our supplies.

"We'll at least celebrate this victory with cold hot dogs," she said.

"What about making a fire, so we can cook them?" George asked. "The scent of victory will reach our enemies!"

"Fire hazard," I said, "and we left our Coleman stove at a fake campsite."

"You two are mysterious!" George extended his arm with his fist balled tight. "I am happy to be a Spartan with you!"

I placed my fist over his, and then Lea put hers on mine. We were three against many, but with only one way to the fort, we had a chance to win.

V

We had left behind the things that made us children. Today, we had become adults—or one step closer, anyway. We talked about making traps, starting with the impossible and working our way to the doable. "We could dig pits and cover them with leaves," I suggested.

"That's stupid." George shook his head. I sensed in his voice the worry that he'd sided with the losing team.

"Okay." I had an edge to my voice. "We could wait for the next attack and run out of ammo."

"We're on the same team," Lea reminded us before George's sigh turned into an insult.

We needed to keep busy to stop ourselves from turning on each other. Lea and I hadn't gotten much sleep the night before due to the watches, so we were tired and cranky.

"How about we just eat lunch and not talk for a while?" George said, glaring at me as he took a hot dog from the cooler. "Is there ketchup?"

"No," I told him, a little ashamed now for being so unprepared. Then Lea got a text.

"It's that kid. Your dad is looking for us in the campground," she said. "How are you going to get to the site?"

"The rules of engagement," I told Lea. "No one can fire on us if a grown-up is present."

This was going to be tricky. If I invited my dad to the treehouse, he'd see we were camping here. But if I asked him to meet me too far away, I'd wind up in enemy territory and get painted. This could easily be game over by either Zeke or my dad.

"Now your dad's texted me. He's at our site."

"Okay, text my dad back and say you and George are at the beach, and I'll meet him at the entrance to the woods."

"How are you going to make it through the trail without running into one of Zeke's sentries?"

"No way Zeke is still nearby. His easy victory was taken from him, so he's probably regrouping. All I have to do is show my dad we're doing fine, and I can get back here."

Lea sent the text.

"Wish me luck," I said and took off my paintball gear. Both Lea and George saluted me, and I cautiously took to the path.

Leaving the treehouse to George and Lea gave me a sense of ease. If Zeke attacked again, Lea wouldn't be alone. But without my gear, I could get tagged out by any of Zeke's team.

I kept an eye on the terrain; to my right were huge heads of skunk cabbage. Zeke would never hide there. But to my left was open forest with fallen trees that were easily seven feet in diameter. A few kids could be behind them, ready to take me out. When I was nearly at the entrance to the woods, Zeke stepped out from behind a tree. He had two Immortals with him.

"Day one, and it's game over for the pukester," he said and raised his weapon. I closed my eyes, ready for the hit.

But before Zeke pulled the trigger, my dad shouted, "Hello!"

Zeke quickly put away his paintball rifle and said hello. I could hear the disappointment in his voice.

"Hey, Dad, so glad to see an adult in the woods," I said, emphasizing the word *adult* so Zeke would remember our rules. "I was just on my way back to the campsite."

My dad looked at me and at the kids with the paintball gear.

"You playing paintball here? Not sure you should be doing that."

"No, sir," Zeke said quickly. "We saw Art on the trail and we invited him to a game."

My dad looked at me. "Why aren't you with Lea?"

"She's at the beach with George. I needed a break from him. He's getting on my last nerve, y'know?"

My dad nodded and I knew he didn't remember George at all.

"Okay, just make sure you have enough food and you're staying warm at night," he said. "I didn't see the cooler or your sleeping bags at your site."

There was an uptick to his voice, so I knew he wanted an answer.

"They stayed at my campsite yesterday," Zeke said. "We had a cookout."

My dad nodded, satisfied with that answer. "Okay." He looked at me. "Do you need anything else?"

A thirty-second head start? I thought as I considered how I was going to get out of this without getting shot once my dad was gone.

"Nope. I'm good," I said.

"Your aunt will be arriving later. Keep that in mind," he said to me.

I had a feeling I was about to be out of the game anyway, so I was going to be free for the rest of the weekend. *Sorry, Lea,* I thought.

"Okay. See you tomorrow, then," my dad said, looking again at Zeke, his friends and then me. He walked down the trail. Zeke blocked the path to my dad, and his two friends were blocking the path behind me.

"Nowhere to run, puke for brains. You weren't even a challenge."

I heard the pop of a paintball, and a kid behind me shouted, "Ow! I got painted!" Then another paintball exploded on a tree near the other kid and another beside Zeke.

"It's a trap!" Zeke shouted.

He and the kid who didn't get tagged leaped into the bush. The one who got shot sulked off down the path in the same direction as my dad. A kid with frizzy brown hair carrying a pack nearly as big as he was emerged from the bushes. I had no idea who he was, but as he walked to my side he said, "You're lucky I happened by when I did."

"Yeah, thanks. How did you know to come?"

"I logged in to that *A.D.* game. Saw your chat about waging a war." He spoke with an old-Western-movie voice. "I aim to share some of my paint with those guys. Payback for all the times Zeke got me kicked out of the water park. I'm Mason."

We walked back to the fort, where Lea and George had been joined by a dozen kids. Some tall skinny kid was yelling about the lack of security and how he would get right on that. Tents were going up around the treehouse.

"Who are you?" I asked the tall skinny kid.

"Evan, sir! I know how to build things!" he shouted and saluted me. He looked up at our sign and mouthed *Sparta*. "We're all Spartans now." He gestured at the dozen kids around him.

"Excuse me, sir?" came a voice from beside me. I looked over and then down to see a kid with thick glasses standing beside me with an iPad.

"Uhh, yeah?"

"Can I interview you and Lea later for a history paper I'm writing?"

"What?" I blinked, as though that added something to my response.

"I'm writing a summer paper about my trip to America. In poetry! My name is Hiroko. Hiroko Dotus."

"Stop!" George shouted. "This isn't your war!"

We all stared at George, wide-eyed, waiting for him to finish.

"Some of you live here all year long, but most of you come for the summer and then you're gone. This isn't your war. This is Lea's war and Art's war. They started it. They decided it was time to defend their right to the water park. This does not concern you, and you should go home—"

I stood face to face with George and held up my hand to stop him from speaking. "No. This is their war every bit as much as it is ours. You think I'm the only summer kid who was ever ridiculed by Zeke or stopped from having fun by someone like him?"

Murmurs of agreement rippled throughout the crowd. "Kids like Zeke exist everywhere. They steal our homework or they flush our heads in toilets."

Now the murmurs turned into a chorus of "Ooh, gross."

"We're not just standing up to Zeke," I said. "We're standing up to every kid who thinks he can boss us around. These kids have the right to be here as much as anyone.

"This is our war!" I yelled, pumping my fist in the air. "It's our turn to take back our freedom! No more are we the weak children alone in the water park, fearing the Immortals. Today, we are warriors! Today, we are Spartans!"

The crowd cheered and pumped their fists. I hoped Zeke would hear these cries—shouts that called for an end to his reign of terror. Shouts that told him he could never win.

Except, unknown to me, there was a traitor in our midst. One soldier who could bring us all down. One even the Oracle could not have warned me of.

M ason had brought ten plastic trash can lids with him. I could see this contribution made him extremely proud, but I couldn't imagine how they were helpful. Other kids had brought folding picnic tables, but almost no one brought food.

"We need to keep our soldiers from getting painted, and we need to advance our troops, not hide behind picnic tables," Mason said, holding up a lid.

"That could work." George grabbed two lids and walked them over to a cluster of kids. He handed one a shield and moved it so it was covering the kid on his left. He then gave the kid on the left a shield and positioned it so she was protecting the kid on her left. I saw exactly what he was doing and ran over to show the soldiers how they could fire from between the shields.

"We march four by four. The two in the centre hold their shields over their heads, the ones on the side protect the sides—"

"Like a turtle shell," Lea shouted from the treehouse, where she was keeping watch. Victory was starting to look imminent. It felt good to find a use for another one of my mom's words.

"Permission to come aboard, sir!" a squeaky voice shouted. I glanced over and saw a lanky girl staring up at the treehouse.

"Permiss—"

"Climb the rope," I interrupted her.

There was a long pause, and then she said, "I can't."

I took a closer look, and sure enough, there was a cast on her right arm.

"Sir!" She stood tall and saluted me, her chest pushing in and out so hard I worried she might collapse.

"You don't have to salute me," I told her.

Lea climbed down from the treehouse.

"Sorry, sir—er, I mean, Mr. Demus and Ms. Nidas. Er, I mean Art Demus and Lea Nidas."

"'Art and Lea' is fine," my fellow general said. I gave Lea a glance that asked if she knew this kid. Lea shrugged, so I knew this was a cottage or campsite kid.

"Hey," George called, "an attack could come at any time. I shouldn't be the only one training these soldiers. Someone wanna come help me?"

Lea looked back at him and blushed. For some reason, I thought about how often those two got to hang out the rest of the year when I wasn't here. Maybe Lea had more in common with George.

"Can you deal with this?" Lea said to me and then ran off to George. I blushed now. I might have been angry.

"What's goin' on?" I asked the lanky girl. "How'd you even know this was happening— and what's your name?"

"Ephie," she said as we stared at one another. At first I thought she was breathing hard because she was trying to catch her breath, but then I realized she was waiting for permission to speak. I nodded, inviting her to continue.

"I'm visiting from Seattle. This morning, I went to the water park and that kid—"

"Zeke?"

"Yeah, Zeke was telling all the kids if they wanted to stay in the water park, they had to side with him. At first, I thought he was cool, but the way he bossed everyone around made me mad.

"I told him to get bent, and he got his brother to kick me out. Said I was splashing kids in the face, which was a total lie. I got paintball gear and tried getting to the treehouse, but Zeke's guards are everywhere. I almost didn't make it."

"So you're not from around here, then." I'd known Zeke for two summers, and we had never gotten along, but this kid was new. Why would Zeke be kicking her out of the water park? He was getting out of control. "But you did get to us. You're here."

"I found something. You need to see it for yourself, sir."

"Can't you just tell me?"

"I have to show you," Ephie said. Perhaps that should have told me how dangerous this was. "If you decide others should know, that's fine. But I think you should see it first."

I slapped her back the way Lea always did mine to show her we were equals. "Okay, we'll come check it out," I said, eager to know what her secret was. Had I understood that her secret could eventually end us, I would not have been so curious.

Why was I curious? It's like when you have a favourite sweater and you notice a thread sticking out. Do you leave it alone or pull and see what happens? Kids, we pull. We pull every time because we have to know where that string leads. And it leads to the same thing. The destruction of the sweater. Every. Time.

I turned to get Lea and saw her laughing with George. We were the three Spartans, but at that moment they were the two Spartans. My budding anger took over any good decision making.

"Let's go," I said.

Ephie took me to the back of our camp, through some bush. The whole time she had this end-of-the-world look in her eyes. As I followed her it didn't occur to me how stupid it was that I hadn't taken someone I could trust.

It was great that so many kids wanted to be involved in our crusade, but we were still only a few against Zeke's army of a dozen more. How would we hold off the next wave of attack? And what if one of our soldiers wanted to get in good with Zeke? Wouldn't they try to deliver Lea or me as the prize?

By the time I realized that Ephie might have been doing just that, I was so far into the bushes that no one would have heard me if I had screamed. Ephie stopped at a place dense with trees and the natural fence of stinging nettles. This cover made our fort a great location for the standoff. The wall of trees and bushes meant Zeke could only attack us from the front.

"It's here. I covered it," Ephie said as she grabbed a thorny bush and moved it aside. If I were a cartoon, my jaw would have dropped to the ground. *A deer trail.* A wide, open trail made by deer. It was new—it had to be—and it left us vulnerable to a flanking attack. From the look of it, the trail led to the campgrounds.

"How many people know about this?"

"Only us, sir," Ephie squeaked back.

"Good. We need to keep it that way. I'm

entrusting, no, deputizing you as the guardian of this path. You'll watch, listen and wait. And we'll pray that Zeke doesn't find out about it."

"One other thing, sir?" Ephie asked and I nodded. "I wanna be a soldier. I wanna be on the front lines."

I looked at the trail and then behind me at the clear sightline to the treehouse. We didn't need another soldier; we needed a guard posted here. I considered how we needed our soldiers to hold a shield with one hand while firing paintballs with the other.

"Soldier, can you hold a paintball gun?"

"Of course, I can carry a paintball gun." Ephie sounded as though my question were like venom in her ears. I didn't want to hurt her feelings, but I had to be realistic. On the front lines, she could get us painted.

"Show me," I said, not because I wanted to embarrass her, but so she could save face. I handed her my weapon. Again, a stupid thing for me to do since no one knew I was here.

She took my paintball gun and pressed the butt against her shoulder. It rested on her hand, but the cast wasn't allowing her to pull the trigger.

"I can shoot with my left," she said and tossed the weapon into her other grip.

I placed my hand gently on her shoulder. "You'd need to hold a shield with your left hand, and your paintball gun in your right. You just can't do it with that cast." When she didn't respond, I said, "Ephie, you can be of extreme use to us here. No one else knows about this path—and no one else can guard it as you can. Holding a paintball gun is no more important than this."

Ephie kicked some dirt and mumbled, "But you guys look so solid."

"Soldier?" I made sure to make eye contact. "We need you here."

She nodded, and I hoped my message had gotten through. This path meant we were no longer cut off. I smiled, foolishly believing this tipped the odds in our favour.

VII

I returned to the camp to find Lea and George laughing and goofing around more than organizing the soldiers like they were supposed to be doing. It upset me they were taking things so casually, or maybe I was upset because that should have been Lea and me laughing and having fun.

Lea ran up to me when she saw me. "Where'd you disappear to?" she asked.

"Surprised you even noticed," I grumbled.

"What?" She gave me a look that told me she was ready to argue. I shrugged it off.

"Do we have a whistle or something loud like that?" I asked.

"Yeah, 'cause I'm a gym teacher."

"I'm serious. We need something loud."

Lea's phone jingled, and she looked at the screen.

"You got a text. Your aunt is in town, and your dad wants you to meet her at the car show at four."

I'd known this was coming, but I hadn't prepared for it. It was going to be next to impossible to get to my aunt without getting hit. I watched George practise with a shield and his paintball gun, and I wondered if he and Lea would become best friends for the rest of the summer if I got taken out today. I had to stay in the game, but how? Ephie's secret path! If her path led to the campsites, I might be able to pull this off.

"Come with me, Lea. I have something to show you."

❖❯❯❯❯❯❖❮❮❮❮❖

"Whoa" was all Lea could say when I took her to the path. She peered in, squinting as if that would give her the ability to see through the shade and twists and turns. "What if they know about it? What if Zeke uses this to send his army to surround us?"

I glanced over at Ephie, who stood tall and kept her eyes on the trail. At that moment, I had no doubt that Ephie would sound an alarm if a rear attack were happening. She was one of us.

"That's why I wanted a whistle. So Ephie could sound an alarm."

"I have my cell phone," Ephie said, holding up her iPhone.

Lea whispered, "The Oracle's playlist." She looked at her phone and scrolled through something. Then she said to Ephie, "Do you have Spotify?"

"Uh, yeah," Ephie said, like she wondered who possibly couldn't have it. I wasn't allowed to have my own cell phone until I turned thirteen.

"Look for a song called 'Eye of the Tiger.' Play it as loud as you can if you see Zeke and his crew." Lea turned to me. "Hey, we could use this for supply runs!" she said, punching my shoulder. "Do we know where it goes?"

I shrugged. "We don't. It might not even go anywhere."

"It could lead to a bear," Lea said.

"Unlikely," I said, though that was possible. "Right now, I'll try to use it to get to my aunt."

"What about her?" Lea nodded at Ephie, who stayed focused on her task.

"She's got our backs," I said loudly enough so that Ephie would hear it. She smiled, and I knew the compliment had hit home. "You should stay here," I added to Lea as we took a couple of steps down the path.

"Yeah, that's happening."

"Seriously, if you come with me and get hit, it's all over. You make these kids think they can beat Zeke. You make them think this stand isn't for nothing."

"George can take care of the team for now. You and I are in this together, and you may need help getting in and out of town. I'm not letting you do this alone."

"Plus, you think my aunt is super cool."

"Duh, she fixes up old cars and dresses like a biker from the fifties. I love her so much!"

"How will I know it's you two returning?" Ephie said as we started down the path.

I raised my eyebrows at Lea, to see if she had any ideas. She shrugged. "We need a signal."

"Bleat like a goat," Ephie told me. I gave her my quizzical look and she added, "There're no goats here in these woods so I won't mistake it for anything else."

"Makes sense," I replied.

I followed after Lea with my weapon slung over my shoulder. At first it was just trail and blue sky above. We heard the wind whistling through trees, the birds fluttering from branch to branch and all that typical nature stuff. For a moment, it felt like any other summer. Except that Lea was carrying her paintball rifle and watching nature through a scope. Made me hope we didn't run into a bear. A bear would not accept the rules of paintball.

"We gotta talk about something," Lea said with an edge to her voice.

"What?" The seriousness in her tone made me nervous.

"You. You know how dumb it was to go off with a kid whose name you didn't even know?"

Lea stopped. She relaxed her weapon, but her face tightened. I shook my head, even though I ultimately agreed.

"I had to, Lea. You couldn't go. You're going to become a symbol, like Batman, but without

77

the gadgets. These kids need you—you're the one who's gonna make them feel like they can accomplish anything. They know you and trust you. If you get painted, it crumbles. We can't let this crumble."

"No way," Lea said. "You and I until the end or this has no meaning. Truth is, you're the one who rallied the kids and kept their spirits up."

I forgot about how angry I was that she was paying so much attention to George.

The trail ended at the campsites, far enough away it wasn't obviously a route to our camp but close enough we could quickly make our way to town. As long as no one saw Lea or me emerging from it, we were golden.

"This changes everything," Lea whispered. Her smile matched my own as we headed to the campsite.

VIII

One good thing about the Birch Bay Rollback Weekend was how busy the town got. People from all over drove around in ancient cars, fixed up from the '80s or '70s or even older. My dad and my aunt loved the weekend. They talked about how they would have loved something like that when they were kids and spending summers in Birch Bay. I always reminded them that when they were kids, those cars weren't "old cars." They were "new cars."

My aunt Sam fixed up old cars as her job. She was pretty cool about most stuff, and Lea liked being around her.

Last summer my aunt Sam had showed Lea how to do an oil change; I thought it was pretty boring, but Lea loved it.

But my aunt did some cool things with me, too, like taking me to water parks in Cultus Lake and then making me feel better after I puked. No doubt she would visit again a few times this summer, but at the Rollback Weekend, everyone treated her like a superstar. She had a really nice car.

"A 1972 'Cuda," Lea said as we skulked through the campsite making sure to stay where we could see a grown-up. Even if Zeke saw us, he couldn't paint us. "Does she still have it?"

I shrugged. "The black car that's got the big hood and super loud engine?" I said. "Yeah, she still has it."

The main road along the shoreline was so busy, cars moved inch by inch. The air was thick with exhaust fumes. The parking lot by the BP Heron Center was full, and families were moving from their cars to the beaches with blankets and chairs.

"Where do you think Zeke is? Where's his home base?"

I shrugged. "I'd guess he's close to home. Someplace comfy."

We stood at the edge of the campsites on the opposite side of the creek from the BP Heron Center. Campers walked over the white bridge in bathing suits with beach towels slung over their shoulders. The summer was alive.

"What's the plan?" Lea asked. "Do we just walk from crowd to crowd until we get to the car show?"

I considered getting Lea to text my aunt to pick us up here, but the main street was going so slow she'd take all day. Plus, my aunt was probably already parked in her spot at the car show and busy showing off her shiny car.

There was a chance my dad would make me stay with the family, maybe even past dinner. Our troops would never last that long without Lea or me there. As much as I didn't want to be out in the open alone, I had to convince Lea to go back. She'd have other chances this summer to see my aunt.

"Lea, you have to go back now. If Zeke sees us both out here, he may take it as a chance to attack our camp. We can't leave this all on George."

Lea started to argue but couldn't finish any sentence she started. She knew I was right.

"I want to see Sam," Lea admitted.

"Aunt Sam will be back another weekend. This is the price we pay."

Lea nodded and sighed. I nodded back and handed her my gear to take with her. "I can't look like I'm at war."

"Don't get painted," Lea said as she punched my shoulder. I watched after her, knowing that while this wasn't how I'd imagined our summer, it was certainly the best we'd had so far. I couldn't believe she'd be gone next year.

⇥>>>><<<<⇤

I stayed deep in the crowds, moving from cluster of grown-ups to cluster of grown-ups. I walked casually, so I'd be less noticeable. The good thing about being a cottage resident was that no one who lived in town really knew me, except the small group of kids I hung out with every year. Lea, the twins, Zeke and George were my summertime cottage group.

I made it to the field where all the old cars were parked. I didn't get why adults put so much work into these giant metallic gas guzzlers. Aunt Sam wasn't even alive when her 'Cuda was first made. The car was older than she was!

I saw her polishing her car. It was shiny, that's for sure. And before I could say anything, I heard a voice behind me.

"Art!"

I turned and saw a brother and sister about my age standing beside a big yellow truck. I had no idea who they were.

"Told you it was him!" the brother said.

"Good luck getting out of here without getting tagged," the sister said, showing me her paintball gun. "You can't hide with the grown-ups forever."

This was exactly what I had worried about. Choosing this weekend to challenge Zeke suddenly felt...my mom's word for this would be "impetuous" or "rash."

"Hey, kiddo!" my aunt shouted at me. I ran to her, and she gave me a big hug. I felt like I was using her as a human shield.

"Hi, Aunt Sam."

A big guy with a beard and tattoos came to look at the car. He read the plaque posted in front of it, and then he looked at my aunt. "When does Sam get here? I have some questions about this ride."

My aunt took a breath first before answering. "*I'm* Sam. This is *my* ride. *I* restored it."

"Oh." The man put up his hands as if in apology and then walked away without asking anything. It was weird.

"Anyway." Aunt Sam looked at me and then around the field. "Where's Lea?"

"Uh, she's busy today," I said. It wasn't a lie exactly. She was busy; I just didn't mention she was busy defending a treehouse from Zeke's army of Immortals.

She nodded as a family started looking at her car. The grandpa was talking about how he bought one brand new when he was in his twenties. He showed us an old photo of himself with a young woman and a few kids.

"They grow up fast." He was interrupted by a woman I assumed was his daughter, who hugged him. They wandered off.

"You doing okay?" Aunt Sam asked. "I heard you had some trouble back home after—"

"—the incident that shall not be spoken of?" I said quickly. Then I added, "Yeah, I'm good."

Aunt Sam kept talking, but my attention was on the crowd. The brother and sister were gone, and I wondered where they were. Did I have a target on me? Was I being watched? Were snipers ready to paint me the second I was alone? Aunt Sam squeezed my shoulder.

"You sure you're okay?"

"Yeah, yeah, good." I needed a plan to get back to the woods. This was not going to end well. Sure, Lea and George could handle things, but I wanted to be a part of it. I wanted to be by Lea's side, winning this thing. I loved my aunt, but I wished I could have waited until another weekend to see her.

"I'm going to get a hot dog, you want one?" she said. As she started walking off, Zeke entered the grounds with the brother and sister. He smiled wide and pointed at me with his fingers like a pistol.

"Y'know, I'm going to come with you." I rushed to get beside her.

"Okayyy…" She looked where I was looking and saw Zeke. "Is that guy bothering you? I can go talk to him. Or his parents."

"No!" I said way too quickly, and my aunt's expression changed from pity to suspicion.

"You tell me what's going on, or I'm going to run as fast as I can over to that hot dog stand. For some reason, you want to be right with me, and I'm one hundred percent sure it has something to do with that scrawny kid over there."

I considered letting her do it and seeing if I could keep up. But my aunt is crazy fast, and there was no way I was going to get out of telling her the truth. Zeke pointed to the opposite side of the field, where I could have made a dash for the woods, and the brother and sister headed there—to cut off the route to the treehouse. I'd have to pass Zeke to get to the road, or the brother and sister to get to the woods. Both ways that led to our secret path were cut off.

"You have five...four...three..."

"Wait! Aargh!" I told her everything—Lea having to move because Zeke's dad bought their house, the Plunge at the water park, the kids finding the video of me puking at Cultus Lake and the agreement to battle it out with paintball.

"Those are good rules," my aunt said and nodded. "I'm impressed you found a constructive way to settle your differences. It's smart to find a way to change the narrative." I should have known I could count on my aunt to understand that paintball was a reasonable solution to a problem.

"If you tell my parents, they'll put a stop to it," I said.

"You aren't giving your parents enough credit. Plus, this puts me in an awkward position."

"What if I agree to tell them when it's over?"

"And if things go too far, you'll call me. Do you have a phone yet?"

I shook my head. "Lea does."

Aunt Sam handed a business card to me. "The second anything goes sour."

I nodded.

"I'll walk you back."

I thanked her profusely, and we walked out of the field. As we passed Zeke, he whispered, "Next time, I'll get you. You can't win this."

IX

As my aunt and I neared our camp, she stopped and looked ahead at the trail. "This good?"

"Yeah."

"You're a smart kid, you'll know if this has gone too far. If you say it's all good, I'm going to trust you."

"Thanks, Aunt Sam."

She turned and left me, and I hurried on. When I got to the treehouse, my people were huddled in groups, all pointing their weapons at the same target. George was at the front talking to three kids who looked familiar.

"Every kid in two counties has joined us,"

said the kid at the front of the trio. "When we shoot, our paintballs will black out the sun!"

"It's such a hot day, we'll be glad for the shade!" Lea said.

"What's going on here?" I shouted as I made my way through the crowd, raising my hand for everyone to hold back.

"I'm a messenger for the Immortals," the front kid told me, puffing his lips importantly.

"You tell Zeke we are no one's subjects," I said. "We are free kids, and we will hold this spot until the Rollback Weekend is done."

"Or when our parents call us to go home," a kid yelled from my group.

"You're crazy," the messenger said. "You can't win this!"

I grabbed a paintball gun and aimed at his chest. "No. We're not crazy. We're SPARTANS!"

I only wanted to rile up my army and get them excited about winning. All we had to do was hold the fort for two more days, and Zeke hadn't attacked since noon. Sending a messenger to ask for our surrender was proof he was scared, proof he knew he might not win this. As long as I could keep my team thinking as one unit, we could do this.

And then someone knocked into me, and I squeezed my trigger. A paintball fired, and I watched as green splatted over the messenger's chest. I glanced over my shoulder and saw the unmistakable upset on Lea's face.

A point-blank shot would have hurt a lot, and it's poor sportsmanship. When you're that close to your enemy, you're supposed to give them the option to surrender.

"Ow!" the messenger said in a voice on the verge of tears. "Aww, man! I got taken out early!" His shoulders slumped and he headed back down the path. The kids who came with him followed on his heels, ready for us to fire on them.

"Prepare for an attack," Lea said to George.

"That was an accident," I said to Lea. "Someone bumped me—"

"I know." She looked around at the kids getting ready for attack. "But was it an accident someone bumped you? I don't know. You need to be in the treehouse. You're the best sniper we have and that's the best vantage point."

I shook my head. "Dude, no way. The best vantage point is on the ground. Behind a shield—"

"True, *if* I wanted you sniping *Zeke's* team."

I couldn't see what Lea was seeing. I yearned for those times long ago when Lea and I were so much alike we could have been siblings. This war was changing us.

"Don't you think it was a bit too easy to gather this army? These kids, do they all want revenge against Zeke? Or do they want to impress him so he'll let them in the water park? Someone bumped you to get you to fire. To paint the messenger."

Lea walked to the treehouse with me and grabbed the climbing rope. She gave our group a good once-over and spent a little too much time watching George.

"You're right," I said. "Someone may want to get in with Zeke. And that paints us with a big target."

War isn't always about heroism and valour. It isn't all about falling on grenades for your pals or pushing your best friend out of the way to take the paint yourself. Sometimes, it's about waiting. And being bored with a capital B. It wouldn't have been so bad if it hadn't got so hot. The air was thick and heavy, like those moments before a big rainstorm. I regretted leaving that tarp in the garage.

And then the first shot was fired. A single bullet, from the woods, paint exploding on the wall behind me. It went right into our window. I crouched to the floor, and so did Lea. Shots fired more rapidly, and then we were once again in the middle of battle.

"Zeke's army is only targeting us," Lea shouted over the pops of paintball guns.

George's voice was our call of rescue. "First wave!" he shouted. Then one giant pop as a dozen paintball guns fired at the same moment. Our people, under George's leadership, must have taken out Zeke's first line because the shooting stopped. When it started again, they no longer targeted the treehouse. They were searching for George!

Lea and I took to the window. Zeke's army was coming down the path in rows of three. They also carried trash can lids, but their metal lids were much smaller than ours. They held them to cover only themselves and lowered them to fire at us.

Lea aimed from the window, raining paint-balls from above. And it looked like rain—an orange and green and purple hail of balls firing so furiously they often exploded mid-air against each other. Nothing could have stopped this. Nothing.

"Samuuuuuuuel," called a woman's voice from down the path. "Samuuuuuuel." The firing stopped as the Immortals made way for the most powerful force in nature: a mom.

"Mom! I told you already I would be here all weekend," said a kid I recognized from the C Shop.

"Oh, Samuel!" she said in one of those mocking scolding tones I often heard from my mom. "You forgot your flashlight! What would happen if you got scared at night?"

"Mooom." Samuel left his post and walked quickly to snatch the flashlight from his mother. He tucked it under his arm and turned to leave.

"Samuel. You know I'm not leaving until I get a kiss."

"This is so why I get beat up," Samuel muttered as he turned back and kissed his mom. Immediately, there were kissing sounds from both armies.

"Now, don't forget to call and let me know you're okay." She turned to leave. As she disappeared from view, she called, "Have fun, kids!"

Then a car door shut. An engine started. There was a crunch of gravel as the car drove away. Once more, paint blasted from both sides.

As in the battle in *Zero A.D.,* Zeke's soldiers were unable to overwhelm us through the narrow path. But the woods proved a better attack point than Lea or I had thought, and several of our team got tagged. As they walked off the battlefield, they saluted toward the treehouse and shouted, "Hoo! Hoo! Hoo!" That became our call.

Zeke's troops had dwindled as ours had, but Zeke's greater numbers meant we'd be done for much sooner.

"Stay in turtle formation!" George shouted, pushing a few forward into a line. But our soldiers were dashing behind the picnic tables or holding their shields in front of themselves, too scared to fire back.

"We need to do something," I said to Lea.

Lea assessed the battlefield, and as a smile spread across her face, she took out her phone.

"The Oracle's playlist will save us," she said. Holding her phone to the window she played a song from Triumph that got my blood going from the first note. "'Never Say Never.'"

As the song got louder, our troops returned to formation. They protected each other with their shields and returned fire. Zeke's soldiers started shouting "I'm tagged!" or "I got painted!" and held their hands over their heads as they left the battlefield.

"We will name that path the Thermopylae Path, and it shall always be remembered as such," Lea said as she paused firing.

Once Lea moved to Seattle, would anyone I hung out with even care about what happened today? I looked at my army with their large plastic shields, working together to stay in the game. Even though we were all fighting side by side, we didn't know each other.

"Fall back! Retreat!"

The call came late in the day, as empty

stomachs and the need for bathroom breaks threatened to destroy us.

But the call didn't come from our side.

Zeke's army was sent home in painted disappointment. I wondered how many might be regretting the side they had chosen. As we heard the rustle of bushes and the retreating steps, the Spartans let out a cheer of victory. "Hoo! Hoo! Hoo!"

A welling of emotions in me made me feel like a balloon with too much air that might pop at any second. I had never felt this way before, and I didn't know what it was. Fear? Anger? I climbed down the rope to the forest floor below.

"Pride," George said as he sidled up beside me. "You're all fidgety like you're trying to crawl out of your own skin—"

"That's gross."

"It's something my mom says to me. Now I know what she means."

He slapped me so hard on the back that I stumbled. "Good work, General. I chose the right team after all."

I wanted to give him a shove in return. He may have been amazing in his duties as frontline commander, but he still wasn't in charge.

When I tried to speak, the words jumbled in my throat. Lea stepped between us, first looking at me and then at him.

"You're both great," she said.

"We need to concentrate on winning the war," I said, once again feeling a weird anger. We'd managed to hold the treehouse, but the war was far from over. With the setting sun, dark clouds rolled in. Rain would come. Cold would follow. And we still needed to feed our troops and keep morale high.

"Get your tents up!" I shouted as I climbed the rope partway to the treehouse. George nodded and immediately made sure every kid had shelter for the night. They needed to stay warm and dry. I climbed the rest of the way into the treehouse and Lea followed.

"I gotta check in with my mom, can I use your phone?" I said to Lea as I held out my hand. "Are you gonna call your dad?"

Lea shook her head, though she probably knew I'd asked just to be polite. Her dad never worried.

As I heard the phone ringing on the other end, Lea looked off into the distance and sighed.

When my mom answered, we chatted about how I was okay and having fun. She liked to baby me. Hearing her voice made not telling her everything that was going on hard. As far as she knew, I was still at the campsite.

Eventually I was mumbling, "C'mon, I don't wanna say that. C'mon, Mom, Lea's here... okay, yeah, I love you." I acted like it was a big inconvenience, but, deep down, I missed my mom. I just needed to get through tomorrow, and we'd be victorious. One more day and I would get away with the biggest lie I had ever told—but there was one more loose cannon.

"Hey, bud," my aunt Sam said on the phone. "Everything still good?"

"Yeah, yeah. All good."

"It's going to rain. You sticking it out?"

I couldn't let the weather break me. Lea and I had come too far, and we'd never have another chance to stand together. Imagining her gone next summer suddenly made me wish the Rollback Weekend would never end.

"I won't give up. There's too much at stake."

"Good. Standing up for what you believe is far better than a summer of video games and potato chips."

I said goodbye and handed the phone back to Lea.

"Maybe we should check with the Oracle's playlist?" Lea said once I was off the phone.

"Really?" My voice peaked in a way that let her know I thought she was crazy.

"Yeah. I'm telling you, the Oracle is wise. We need to listen to what it wants us to do."

I rolled my eyes at her; she had completely lost it. Lea ignored me and opened Spotify on her phone. She tapped a few times and turned up the volume. A high-pitched scratchy voice sang about how nothing lasts forever and it's raining in November.

"It's 'November Rain' by someone called Guns N' Roses," Lea said.

The song seemed pointless and silly at first, and I wondered how Lea could have thought the Oracle's playlist could ever guide us. But, as sometimes happens, there was a moment when it all made sense.

The Oracle spoke to us through song, and we glanced down at our army. George was making one last check on all the kids. He stopped, as though feeling our eyes on him, and turned to meet Lea's gaze. They held until Lea blushed, they smiled and then George continued checking on the kids as the rain started.

"See? Prophetic," Lea said as she closed the drapes on the window.

When someone began climbing up, we missed a prophetic line in the music warning about friends who are out to harm you.

Had we heard that last part of the song, had we been listening, our war might have ended differently.

George poked his head into the fort. "Just wanted to tell you all the kids are in their beds. We have no sentries posted, but it's unlikely we'll get attacked in this rain."

Lea nodded. "Come on in, soldier. Take refuge from the weather."

I stuck my finger in my throat and pretended to gag. She kicked me as she shuffled over to make room. George plopped down beside her, sopping wet. He leaned his weapon against the wall.

"What now, General?" he asked.

"We have a plan," I said through gritted teeth. George's suggestion that we didn't know what we were doing annoyed me—even though we really didn't know what we were doing.

George stared at Lea with a wry smile that made me feel as though they were a team without me. Like they had a secret language the way my parents did. I tried to say something, but for some reason my mouth went all dry and the words choked in my throat. I couldn't figure out what was happening to me.

"You may want to share your plan. The soldiers are talking about going home. The rain, as they put it, sucks."

I cleared my throat loudly until I got my voice back. "In the morning. We'll give them a speech that will inspire them to stay."

"No," Lea said. "We'll tell them if they're cold and tired they should go home."

George gave me a look that told me he didn't get what Lea was saying. I didn't either, so I gave that same look to Lea.

"Those who want to win should understand what a Spartan wants most in life is victory. And victory means standing up for yourself— even when you're cold and wet."

George turned to me and our eyes locked. George always stood up for his friends, and that included me. I needed to get over feeling jealous that he got to spend the whole year hanging out with Lea. That didn't mean she liked him better. After all, Lea had agreed to make this stand with me—even after she found out I was the kid who puked.

XI

The next day, with the rain coming down on us, Lea and I decided to take the secret path to the highway. Paintballs don't shoot well in heavy downpours, so there wasn't a big chance of battle. Going into town was risky—if we were seen, Zeke would know there was another way into our camp and he'd seek it out. Even with an honest soldier like Ephie guarding the entry, if an army took to the path we'd be in trouble.

Lea and I carried only paintball pistols under our hoodies so no one in town would ask about the war.

I hadn't told George about the path, but that

was more in case he was ever caught. The less people knew, the better chance secrets stayed secret.

Plus, I'll be honest, I liked that this was something kept between Lea and me.

We headed straight for my house. Between the two of us, we figured, we'd be able to carry enough supplies to make things comfortable for everyone.

All we had to do was convince our army to stay one last day, and Zeke would lose the war. The Immortals would have no place to swim, while the Spartans reigned over the water park and private beach. Thinking about Zeke swimming on a crowded beach made me chuckle.

"What's so funny?" Lea asked as we climbed the steps to my front porch. I shrugged and walked inside, smelling the aroma of fresh baking. On rainy summer days, my mom buried her nose in a book while my dad puttered around in the kitchen. Today, it smelled like cinnamon buns.

I considered collapsing on the couch with a giant, gooey bun cut open with melted butter in the middle. I was tired. But so were my soldiers, and we had to get back to them.

"You kids want some lunch?" my dad asked as he walked out of the kitchen, covered in flour. He had on his apron that said "01100111 - 01100101 - 01100101 - 01101011." He thought it was hilarious, but I didn't get binary code.

"No, Dad. We're fine," I said, looking away in case my facial expression revealed how much I wanted to say yes.

"Okay. Your aunt just left, by the way."

"Oh. That means we can take the tarp?"

My dad nodded. Lea and I headed toward the garage with my dad close behind. "If it's getting too cold, why not come home? If not, take the extra blankets." I detected a little concern in his tone.

Total score. Then Lea went for the gold. "What about food? Can we take some more food?"

There was a sigh, and my dad fished in his pockets until he pulled out a twenty. "How did you two eat all the food already? Stop in at the store, get something healthier than marshmallows."

"Thanks, Dad."

"And Lea?"

"Yes, sir," she said.

"Your dad called. I told him where you were. He's heading out today on a fishing trip with your brothers; I told him I'd look after you until he gets back."

"Solid," Lea said, but I sensed the disappointment that her dad had only called to say he'd be gone.

"Dude, come on."

There was urgency in my voice now. We'd been gone awhile—maybe too long. The rain was still falling but was letting up enough that the battle could start at any time.

"George can take care of things. Relax."

We grabbed my dad's old hockey bag and ignored the odour of sweaty feet as we filled it with blankets and a tarp. The tarp my aunt used for her car was big enough to cover many of the tents, so our soldiers wouldn't have to stay huddled inside their tents. This was key, I knew.

I saw my dad's Spartan paintball helmet and thought about the ones Lea and I wore. George kept the troops organized and well trained, and I felt bad that my temper was so short with him. I took the helmet with me so that I could officially make him a Spartan leader.

Next stop was the store. But what if Zeke or an Immortal spotted us? How would we possibly make it out alive? But without food, our army was not going to stick around. The store was a chance we had to take.

XII

There it was, Beachwood Grocery and Deli. The one place in town where you could pick up food, camping gear and fishing tackle. It was nestled by an RV park. The gravel parking lot lot was empty, except for a couple of bikes lying on the ground.

"Could be Zeke's people," Lea whispered. "They see us, they'll report back."

I didn't say anything at first. We had to get in there and buy supplies. Not only canned food to last the rest of the weekend, but also cookies and chips to boost morale. This shop—and the sweet treats it could provide—was the difference between winning and losing this war.

"Do you think we should have sent someone less recognizable?" I said.

We both knew if we'd sent someone less recognizable, we'd have sent someone we didn't know we could trust. One more person would know about Ephie's path, and they'd probably never return with our supplies or our money.

"Get in and get out. We need to be quick." Lea headed for the parking lot, walking boldly across the gravel.

We tried to peek in through the big front window to see if we could spot the owners of the bikes. If they were Zeke's crew, we could wait until they left. Trouble was, in this small town there wasn't much else to do other than bike to the general store. They could be in there for ages.

I didn't spot anyone, and I assumed by Lea's continued walk to the door that she didn't either. Lea grabbed the door handle first, but I grabbed her hand to stop her.

"No. I should go in first. If things go sour, you need to run. Don't worry about me—the cause is all that matters. You must protect the treehouse."

She nodded.

"If I do get tagged"—Lea spoke as though she expected not to make it—"I'll be proud to get painted by your side."

I walked through the door and answered, "I'll be happier living by yours."

The bell dinged and Mr. Chan saw us and smiled. We smiled back and, grabbing a basket, headed straight for the canned goods aisle. We didn't see anyone until we'd half filled our basket with canned stew and tuna.

"Lookey-lookey," came a voice.

"If it ain't the—"

"—Spartans. Where's your—"

"—army?" It was the twins.

I glanced at Lea, wondering if we should run. The last thing we needed was these two blabbing we were here. The first time Zeke saw me away from the treehouse, he probably assumed I had snuck down the path and got lucky. But he'd soon realize there was a secret way in and out. And he'd stop at nothing to find it.

"You two choose a side?" Lea spoke first and raised her paintball gun.

The twins smiled and their eyes went wide.

"You gonna shoot—"

"—us here? In the store?"

I pushed Lea's muzzle so it pointed to the ground. "We abide by the rules of the game."

"Shut up!" one of the twins demanded. I placed my finger on my trigger. The twins looked around, their heads bobbing like roosters.

"They're coming. You two gotta—"

"—hide. Go to the frozen veggie—"

"—section. Zeke never goes there."

Zeke? Then I heard a door slamming outside. Zeke was climbing out of the passenger side of his dad's truck. *He's here!* For supplies, no doubt.

"The rules. We're safe, right?" Lea asked.

"Zeke can wait for us to leave. Eventually we have to try and get back to the treehouse."

Lea grabbed my arm and dragged me to the frozen vegetable section, the safest aisle. What kid in his right mind would pick vegetables over candy? We crouched down low, aware that Mr. Chan was watching us in his theft mirror. *Please don't call us out, Mr. Chan.*

A ding at the door signalled Zeke's entry. I listened to his footsteps as they clomped into the candy aisle—as expected. And then I listened, far more intently, as the twins wandered over to Zeke.

"What you guys hear? My ginger spies bring me anything good?"

Lea's glare said exactly what I was thinking: *They're on his side!*

We prepared for capture. Even if Zeke couldn't shoot us in here, he'd definitely wait us out.

"We've seen—" one twin began, and Lea and I gripped our paintball guns tighter, waiting for the other twin to finish.

"—nothing." The sound of a slap on the back followed the twins' words, and then wrappers crunched as candy was gathered.

"You've done well."

Then more footsteps. The ringing of the cash register. The doorbell's jingle.

We stayed put until we heard the truck driving off.

Had we really just survived such a close encounter? Lea brought her fingers to her lips, signalling me to be silent. She peered around the aisle, took a couple of steps out, then waved for me to follow. All was clear.

"Why?" Lea asked one of the twins.

"Isn't it—"

"—obvious?"

I looked to Lea, who looked to me, and then we both shook our heads. No, it wasn't obvious.

"We're tired of Zeke—"

"—telling us when to jump and—"

"—how high to jump. You have a chance—"

"—to take away his power."

I nodded. I understood what they were talking about. Freedom: it's what a Spartan stood for. Every kid should be equal and stand together. We immediately started gathering supplies and stopped wasting time. Even if Zeke didn't come back, we could still be outed by one of his team. Our trip to town needed to stay secret.

"If you tell us where—"

"—your secret way into town is—"

"—we can bring you what you need."

The register beeped as Lea paid for our supplies. She wasn't within earshot, so this was my decision. Did I let these kids in on our secret?

"I appreciate what you two have done," I said, choosing my words carefully. I knew this could be a trap. Why tell Zeke we were there, when you could wait to deliver the ultimate secret? One that would completely destroy us.

"Knowing our way in would put you in

danger and make you a target for Zeke. I can't have that on my conscience."

The look they gave one another told me they were disappointed. Whether it was disappointment that I hadn't let them in as allies or that now they had nothing for Zeke I wasn't sure. Lea whistled for us to get away while we could.

"Thanks. I won't forget your kindness."

They said nothing more as I left, and the eerie silence suggested that they had darker motives than they had let on. I felt I had made the right decision—perhaps back at the fort, I could consult the Oracle to know for sure.

XIII

By late afternoon the sun came out and dried up most of the town, but our feet stuck in the mud and whenever we hit an overhanging tree branch, water sprayed all over us. Staying silent while walking a narrow path through the woods was difficult. Our hands were full of plastic grocery bags and my dad's hockey bag filled with gear. At one point a branch caught a plastic bag, ripping it open and spilling our food in the mud.

"Now what?" Lea said as she stared longingly at the meat cans and candy bars. I hefted the hockey bag onto the ground and unzipped it.

"Let's hope these fit." And thankfully, there was just enough room in the hockey bag.

I was so happy when we finally got near the base.

"Hold up, we need to give Ephie the signal," Lea said.

I called out, "Baaaa."

"That's a sheep, doofus," Lea said. It had never occurred to me I didn't know what a goat sounded like.

"What does a goat sound like?" I asked.

She made a noise that was exactly like the one I'd made, and I told her so.

"That was not the same as yours," she insisted.

"Exactly the same. Seriously. Ephie is not going to know it's us, and she's going to sound the alarm."

At that moment, it occurred to me that even if Ephie did sound the alarm, none of the kids at the fort would know what it meant.

"No, she isn't," Lea said. I looked to where she was looking and saw Ephie standing guard at the mouth of the path.

"That's sheep, not goats," Ephie told us.

"Me or him?" Lea asked.

"Both a' you. You need to bleat. You never heard a goat before?" Ephie made a sound to teach us. It still sounded like the noises we'd been making.

"Okay, thanks," I said. There was no point in arguing with the kid guarding the secret entry to our base.

"And you're so loud, how do you know you weren't followed?"

Before I could answer, I heard a clamour coming from the treehouse. Lea and I dropped our bags and ran for it. We hit so many puddles on the way that when we got to the fort we looked as though we'd been mud wrestling.

George and a bunch of kids were carrying picnic tables to where Lea and I had run from. Hiroko Dotus was taking notes on her iPad. All I could think was, *Great. Now more kids know about the secret pass.*

"Don't be mad," George said. "I followed you and Lea. When I saw you two go into the path, I thought we needed some sort of barricade. We could build a wall of picnic tables and leave a garrison here to protect it."

"Good job, George," Lea said.

"Good job? George, do you understand what

you've done? You just told every kid about our secret path. EVERY. KID." I stormed off. All my soldiers were staring at me, including Ephie.

I knew that George had done the right thing. Not only did this secure a weak spot in our defence, it also gave Ephie some friends to hang out with. But no matter how much I wanted to like George, everything he did rubbed me the wrong way. Like when you pet a cat, and at first the cat likes it but then *WHAM!* the claws come out and you're bleeding. The cat looks at you like it has no idea why it attacked you. George made me feel like the cat.

When I got to the treehouse, Lea brushed past me with the food. She started dividing it up, so I gathered a few kids to set up the tarp. With the sun out again and fresh supplies, hopefully spirits would soar. Lea was glaring at me, and I realized we needed to make amends if we expected our troops to stay a team. That meant I had to apologize to George.

"Who wants a hot dog?" Lea called and was met with a raucous cheer.

"I do, too," said an unfamiliar voice. One of Zeke's people emerged from the Thermopylae Path.

It was the messenger we'd painted yesterday!

"You're painted!" Lea said, pointing her paintball rifle at him.

"Hear him out," I said sternly, and Lea stood down. She gave me that glare again.

"Yes, hear me out," the messenger said, "and you will learn that I am a twin, and I have not been painted!"

Lea and I looked at each other and accepted the twin excuse. It went against the rules about being painted, but the kid wasn't carrying a weapon. He was no danger to us.

"Zeke wants a meeting with Lea and Art. A discussion for peace."

"No," I said for us. Lea patted my back and stepped forward.

"Has he promised our safety there and back?" she asked.

"Of course," the messenger answered.

"Let us confer," I said to the messenger. I guided George and Lea over to the treehouse where we could talk.

"We're not walking into this trap," I said. We'd had so many close calls, I didn't want to push our luck. "We only have to make it to tomorrow morning and this war is over anyway."

"Look at how tired our soldiers are," Lea said. "We have to do this."

"I'll go with you," George said.

"You need to stay here to be in charge," I said. "You're smart and a good soldier. We need you here. This is more than a treehouse; this is their freedom. If Lea and I get painted, you need to lead these kids to victory."

I couldn't look him in the eyes, but I hoped he understood my words to be an apology. "In case we don't come back I want to give you this." I handed him the extra Spartan helmet. Lea punched my shoulder.

I ignored Lea's approval; this was between George and me. "You're a Spartan the same as Lea and me. No matter what, we are the three Spartans!"

I held out my fist, and Lea slammed hers on mine, and George slammed his on ours.

"Why go if there's a chance you won't come back?" asked George.

"You think Zeke's soldiers are fighting out of loyalty?" said Lea. "They fight from fear. We need to tell them there is a better army."

"You think they'll join us?" I asked.

"No. But they might not fight us as hard."

I walked to the messenger and saw he had brought soldiers with him. They were close enough to shoot us if we'd tried to take out a second messenger. I nodded and they came forward to walk us to Zeke's camp.

I looked over my shoulder at my troops, and there was George, watching us with sad eyes. I hoped I'd return to battle by his side without feeling this jealousy. Lea took out her phone, tapped on it and shouted, "Follow the Oracle's playlist!" It started playing "Sharp Dressed Man."

As the song played, George put on his new Spartan helmet. "Hoo! Hoo! Hoo!" he shouted and saluted as we disappeared down the path.

⇥⟫⟫⟫⟩•⟨⟨⟨⟨⟨⇤

Zeke had a group campsite in the park and was sitting on a picnic table. As many as twenty-four tents were up in the site. I had to concentrate to hide how impressed I was by the size of his army. If they were sleeping four or five to a tent, Zeke might have more than a hundred soldiers. I reminded myself that the Thermopylae Path was the only known way in and that the secret pass was now well guarded. Even with his numbers, Zeke had a near-impossible chance of overwhelming us. Zeke had a guard positioned on either side of him.

"Lea, Art, I am glad you have come." He clapped his hands and a bunch of kids carried over another picnic table. A second group of kids behind them filled the table with hot dogs, hamburgers and chips. "You must be hungry. Please, eat."

"No, thanks, Zeke," Lea said. "What do you want?"

"I want us to stop fighting each other. Why should our armies battle, when we could rule together?"

I looked around. No one was having fun, no one looked like they wanted to be there.

"Lea, Art will be going home after the summer is over. You and I shouldn't be enemies, we should be friends. When school starts again, we could rule those halls!"

Lea looked away quickly. I realized she hadn't told any of the other kids she was leaving at the end of summer. Zeke knew his dad had bought their house, but he must have assumed Lea's dad was going to buy another one in Birch Bay. Zeke didn't understand that his dad's desire to own everything had ruined things for Lea.

"Well, with me in charge, of course," Zeke said. "For the summer, I'd give you a section of the water park to rule over. You can decide what kids get to use it."

"We won yesterday's battle. You think you're gonna lose." Lea gave me a look that said she believed this war was as good as won.

Zeke laughed. He hopped off the table and walked over to us. While he towered over me by a lot, he only did a little over Lea. I found myself freezing up while Lea balled her fists.

"Look at the size of my army. You are a fraction of what I am. If you don't agree to this, tonight we slaughter you. Come on, Lea. All you have to do is admit I'm king of the water park and bend your knee."

"I would, but these are my last pair of clean pants and kneeling would get them dirty."

Some of Zeke's soldiers overheard and chortled. Zeke picked up a paintball rifle and tagged a few of them in the chest.

"Maybe I should paint you now and end it!" he said to us.

"Do you think we would have come if we thought you could end our stand by tagging us? If you paint us now, our soldiers will be more determined to win than ever," I said.

"We Spartans have a strong chance for victory," I added, "but we'd be willing to share the water park. All we ask is that no kid, regardless of the side they fought on, be turned away or bothered again."

For a second, Zeke looked like he was considering it. "Only if Art does the Plunge. You either win the war, or Art gets back on that slide."

The one thing I couldn't do. Even thinking about the slide made my stomach churn.

"No," I said, embarrassment creeping into me. Lea punched my shoulder and I knew she was okay with this.

"Fine. Then tonight, we take your Spartans! Tonight, I send my Immortals," Zeke said.

"Come and try!" Lea replied as a challenge, and together we started back toward the treehouse.

XIV

As we emerged from the Thermopylae Path our soldiers applauded. I think they were surprised to see us returning safely. George ran to us first, checking us over by grabbing our shirts and spinning us around.

"No paint. It wasn't a trap?" he asked.

"Nope. He wanted to make a deal," Lea said.

"Tell me everything that happened in detail. For my history report," Hiroko said as she started tapping on her iPad.

They all wanted to know what had happened, and I wondered if they all hoped we'd made a deal. Lea walked to the centre and climbed onto a picnic table so all could hear her.

"Spartans, you look to me with weary eyes that want to go home. You look tired of battle and in need of rest in your own beds. To you I say, go home!"

"What are you doing?" George rushed to her side. I knew she was doing exactly what we had talked about last night. Zeke outnumbered us, and while it didn't look like rain again, this was the Pacific Northwest—it could rain anytime. Soldiers with only half a heart in this battle were more likely to help us lose than win.

"You are not bound to us like Zeke's soldiers are bound to him," I said as I climbed to stand beside Lea. Whatever rift we may have felt earlier was gone. We were best friends, even if we wound up being the only ones to stand against Zeke.

"We don't demand you stay. You're here because you believe in living free, and this is your chance to fight for your freedom. Do you want Zeke to kick you out of the water park, laughing while you cry? Or do you want to know that on this day, you stood for something? You stood for your right to slide in the water. To have fun without having to look over your shoulder. Isn't that what you want?"

127

My voice raised in expectation of cheers, but I got nothing.

"I think we're just tired," a kid said.

"I know I am." Another kid said this as he swallowed a cold hot dog he was stuffing into his mouth. My heart began to sink.

"I'm tired of getting picked on," said George. "I'm tired of Zeke getting everything he wants. You guys can go home, but I'm staying with Lea and Art."

The story I wish I could tell is one where every kid dedicated himself to the cause. Where my words were so inspiring that no amount of cold rain or hot sunny days or spiders crawling into our sleeping bags could drive my people away. But almost all the kids packed up their things. I could have counted those who stayed on one hand.

"I'm not gonna lie, I saw this going down differently," George said as he started picking up trash they left behind. "I thought more kids would stay."

"Why'd you stay?" I asked George.

"You two started something amazing. Do you even get how important it is that we win this?"

"What do we do now, George?" I asked.

"We take those few kids we've got left and go to war."

He was right. Even though we'd likely be slaughtered, and Zeke would win the tree-house. "Maybe," I said, "what these kids need to see isn't winning or losing, but the simple act of standing up to those who oppress us."

"Yup," George said with a full smile as he reached out to squeeze my shoulder.

We headed for one last look at the secret path. There was no point in anyone watching full-time since Zeke didn't know about it. With even Ephie gone, we needed all our soldiers defending the treehouse. George and I walked back to the fort silently, the sun glinting on all the tiny raindrops that still clung to the leaves and knee-high blades of grass. It was like walking through a magical, sparkling world from one of those fantasy books my parents were always trying to get me to read.

By dinnertime, all the tents were gone. The tables were still on their sides, but Mason had taken most of the trash can lids we were using as shields. Dried-up blotches of orange, purple and green paint clung to the trees, bushes and our tables. *This is what defeat looks like,*

I realized. I climbed the rope into the fort with George behind me.

"Did anyone wind up staying?" I asked Lea.

"Nope. The rest took off."

George closed his eyes and sighed. In Lea's voice, I had heard a desire to quit and go home. Had she forgotten how this started? With only her and me? Had George forgotten that when he joined us, there were only three of us?

"It's perfect," I said. Then I slapped Lea on the back and exclaimed, "This is how it always should have been!"

I leaped out of the treehouse so fast I almost lost my grip on the rope as I lowered myself to the ground. I swung so my feet landed firmly and loudly on a picnic table, and Lea quickly followed with George. Both of them gave me sidelong glances that let me know they thought I was crazy.

"We are the only ones left," I shouted loudly, "but there was only ever us."

"We had five times this many kids this morning!" George interrupted me. It was exactly the response I wanted.

"Spartans! We are Spartans! We are soldiers! This is our mission! This is a war we will remember until the end of days. Not because we pulled off an easy win—but because we refused to give up! Zeke may take this treehouse, but we won't hand it to him! If he wants it, he will have to take it from us!"

"Yay?" Lea said. This was not the inspired cheer I had hoped for. What could I do to make her understand we could end the bullying forever for every kid in Birch Bay? I was about to speak again but stopped when I saw George smiling and nodding.

"He's right, Lea," George said, climbing to stand on the table with me. "This is the stand of the three Spartans! No matter what happens, kids will speak of this moment forever. The summer we stood up—"

"—for ourselves?" Lea asked.

"No," George said. "For each other."

XV

That evening, our last of the challenge, George, Lea and I strategized. We made sure the area between the treehouse and the path was clear of tables or anything the Immortals could take cover behind. Then we sat up in the treehouse, with one of us watching the woods through the window at all times. We would be ready for whatever happened.

"As long as Zeke doesn't find the secret path, there's no way he can get his large army to us." I paused to meet the eyes of my generals. "George and I will hold shields on the right and left, so if he comes through the woods we're protected. Lea, you face the path with your shield. It won't matter if there's thirty or three hundred. They'll have to come at us in small numbers—small enough we can pick them off."

George put his hand on my shoulder and I stopped talking. "You sound like you think you're not going home covered in paint," he said.

"I think it's possible," I told him plainly. Then I looked at Lea. "I think we can do this."

There was a beat of a drum from outside. *Boom! Boom! Boom!* And we knew they were coming. This wasn't a sneak attack; this was Zeke telling us he thought victory was his.

"It's time," Lea said. We readied for the attack, swinging on the rope to the ground below and grabbing our shields.

Boom! Boom! The sound of drumming rustled the leaves in the woods. The *boom boom* continued as we waited for the Immortals to show themselves.

They came at us in twos, dressed in purple swim trunks with helmets covering their faces. When one was shot, there was another right behind. Their advance on our ranks through the Thermopylae Path pushed our sharpshooting to its limits, and I heard, above the splatter of paintballs on metal shields, the chatter of an enemy that thought they'd already won.

"Push!" I shouted to George and Lea as we moved forward. When our shields hit the Immortals, there was a stalemate of one wave stopping the other. But the Immortals could only come down the path in threes. George and I pushed them back to the woods and fired on them until they were no more. They lost with whimpers of "Oh, man!" and "I got hit by a nerd!" But still they lost. For a moment, with no Immortals left on the Thermopylae Path, I felt as though we might win this.

But a single pop from behind, a stray purple paintball fired from the back of the treehouse, and George yelled, "I'm hit!"

The rest of Zeke's army ambushed us from the secret path. That was why the assault from the Thermopylae Path stopped.

I dashed for the treehouse, hearing Lea's footfalls behind me. Taking to the rope, I climbed to the top. Once inside, I shut the drapes and pressed my body into a corner, clutching my weapon to my chest.

Paintballs blasted through the thin drapes.

Lea wasn't behind me, and I knew if she hadn't been caught already, it was only a matter of time. I wasn't ready to give up. Not yet. But the unthinkable was true. There had been a traitor among us.

"Art!" Lea cried out. "Are you alive?"

I dared a look out the window, and between two picnic tables, Lea was doing her best to stave off the attack from the Immortals.

"I'm alive!" I screamed, and then before I could talk myself out of it, I leaped out the door and swung on the rope to land beside her. Paintballs flew around me, but not one made contact.

"I thought you were painted," she said as we settled in back to back. My cheeks felt like they were on fire—I was glad she didn't see me blushing.

"It's just us!" I said to Lea.

"I'll stay until the end—to fight for you."

I fired at the Immortals from one side, while Lea fired from hers. Our ammo was running out fast, and I knew we couldn't hold out much longer.

"We lost the war," I whispered as Lea reloaded her paintball gun.

Maybe I hoped she couldn't hear me.

"You have to escape, Art. You have to get out and tell everyone what happened here."

"What are you talking about? Keep firing!"

"No!" She put her hand on my shoulder and smiled as our eyes met. If I was a good leader, it was because I was inspired to be one. It was because Lea inspired me to be better. "You're going to sneak away."

The shooting suddenly stopped. We heard the drumming again, and I knew who'd come. I peered over the picnic table, and there was Zeke, carried on the shoulders of his grunts. Immortals stood on guard around him. None of his followers looked happy. None looked to him the way ours had looked to me and Lea and George.

"You have one last chance," Zeke said loudly, perhaps so he'd be heard by anyone left hiding in the woods. "Surrender to me, and I will spare you."

"No!" Lea grabbed my shoulder.

"It's a good end, Lea."

She let go of my shoulder, and her lower lip stiffened. She held her chin high and nodded once. I turned to get ready to run, but before

I did, she punched my shoulder. As I felt the burning return in my face, I saw a glimpse of a smile from her.

I held my weapon high over my head, and I stepped onto the picnic table. I watched Lea stand, and then I dashed for the woods, hoping I'd be unseen as every eye would be on Lea. The Immortals all loaded their paintball guns and pointed them at her. Zeke smiled, a look of victory piercing my spirit. I paused in the bushes long enough to watch what happened next.

"On your knees."

Lea shook her head no, and I had just enough time to aim my weapon and get out one paintball. It missed Zeke but got so close he must've felt the wind. The Immortals fired on me in the woods and at Lea by our treehouse. Paint spattered off my chest all over the ground around me. Lea and I fell to our knees, but not from loyalty to Zeke. We fell from loyalty to our army. From loyalty to this one last stand.

XVI

When I woke the next day, my legs hurt from all the running, and I had tiny welts on my shoulders and chest from the paintballs. But my injuries made me feel good because I'd stood up for what was right. Plus, as my aunt Sam had said, I "changed the narrative." No one would think of me as "that kid who puked at the water park." Now I was "that kid who challenged Zeke to a paintball war."

My dad was making breakfast—no doubt English muffins with eggs and bacon. I dragged myself out of bed and considered turning on my laptop to log in to *Zero A.D.*, but after spending three days in the real thing I didn't feel like it. I decided to join my parents in the dining room.

"Good morning. Did you and Lea have fun camping?" my mom asked with her eyes buried in what looked like the final chapters of her novel.

"It was okay," I said in a way that discouraged further conversation. I didn't want to lie anymore about it. I had, however, made a promise to my aunt.

"I have to tell you something, and you might be mad. I wasn't exactly at the campsite."

My dad put a plate in front of me and sat. My mom put down her book and came to sit at the table. My dad clasped his hands on the table in front of him; he scrunched his face in a serious expression. I took a deep breath.

"Lea and I had some trouble with a kid at the water park. We challenged him to a game of paintball. I've been at the treehouse in the woods. Sorry I lied."

Neither of them spoke. It was agony waiting for them to yell at me or punish me.

"We know," my mom said. "Aunt Sam told us. She said that she talked to you and that you were with a big group of kids and that you were being smart and safe. She also told us what happened at Cultus Lake and about the video. You should have told us about that. I got the video taken down."

My parents were being great, and now I wished I'd told them about it from the start. I mumbled thanks.

"You will be punished," my mom said. "To start, you and Lea will clean up that treehouse. And there will be more after the summer. You'll have extra chores and maybe you'll volunteer on a cleanup at Finn Slough."

I gave them my confused look where I raise an eyebrow and the corner of my lips.

"This is your last summer with Lea," my dad said. "We're not taking that away. But we expect you to be honest with us the rest of the summer, is that clear?"

"Yes," I said and hugged them both hard.

"Speaking of Lea, she called while you were still asleep. She wants you to call her back," my dad said.

"Okay. I think I'll ride out to that treehouse first, and see what we'll need to do."

I got dressed and ate fast so I could get back out on the road. I wanted to see the fort in the daylight without the troops, without the paintballs and without the war. I needed to see that Zeke had taken Sparta from us and that this really was over.

I grabbed my coat and walked outside into the rainfall, riding my bike down the now quiet main strip.

I rode to the campsite. My tent and camping gear were now packed up and gone, so I assumed George and Lea had been by earlier.

I took the road to the Thermopylae Path. I parked my bike and walked the path, listening to the squish my shoes made in the wet mud. All the paint from our battle was washing off. It almost looked as though we had never been here. Would anyone remember the stand we made?

When I got to the treehouse, I saw the ladder had been put back and Lea was inside, leaning on her hands at the window and staring out. I climbed the ladder to join her inside.

Lea didn't turn to me, she just shrugged. "That was epic, Art," she said.

I sidled up beside her, looking out into the forest as the winds whipped through the trees.

"Any regrets?" she asked.

"You stood by my side, Lea. When all the other kids were ready to write me off as 'the kid who puked,' you accepted me. You're my best friend, and I have no regrets."

The rain let up and a ray of sunshine broke through the canopy of trees. It ignited the songs of all the birds and sparkled in droplets on the leaves.

Lea looked at me and smiled. We may have wanted to win more than anything, but we did have this one thing that Zeke could never take from us: our friendship.

"You still have to do one last thing, Art. And you can do it, because you are the bravest person I know."

I knew what she meant. I needed to do the Plunge. Because this weekend showed I could overcome anything. Even this.

And if I did it, we'd win our deal with Zeke.

"Even if everyone goes back to calling me 'the pukester'?"

"We won't call you that," George said as he climbed the ladder into the treehouse.

"Your dad said you'd be here."

I put out my fist and Lea put hers on mine. Then George put his on ours, and we shouted,

"Hoo! Hoo! Hoo!" like the Spartans. I no longer felt jealous that George got to hang out with Lea all year. Well, not as jealous.

"The sun is out; let's go conquer those slides," I said.

As the three Spartans, we rode our bikes through the campsites, by the beaches and down the main strip, passing kids who had once fought with us or against us. Our first stop was my place, where I changed into swim trunks and found a pair for George to wear. Lea had brought her own, expecting that we'd be going to the water park. It showed me how much she believed in me. Now that we were ready, we rode to the waterslides and put our bikes in the rack. We stood outside the gates.

"Do we have enough money to get in, or do we need the twins?" Lea asked.

This time, I had cash so I paid for the three of us. We pushed our way through the crowds and found our way to the foot of the Plunge. I looked up, sixty feet up to be exact, and my stomach churned a little.

"You got this," Lea said as she punched my shoulder.

"We're with you," George added as he punched my other shoulder.

"Hey, pukester, either you're breaking our agreement or you're here to do the Plunge. Which is it, chicken?"

Again, a crowd of kids surrounded me. Unlike last week, they weren't strangers. These were kids I had stood on the field of battle with. Mason, Hiroko and an Ephie who couldn't meet my gaze were all here. That was how I knew this slide was more important than anything any kid had ever done in Birch Bay.

"I'm here for the Plunge," I said as a chorus of "Hoo! Hoo! Hoo!" broke over the park.

I took to the stairs, and my legs wobbled. While I wanted to be confident and walk up to the top and do the slide with arms raised in triumph, my breath was getting stuck in my chest.

"I'm still with you, Art," Lea said as she and George took the stairs with me.

"I can't, Lea, I'm sorry. I wanted to be a leader, but Zeke is right. I'm just the puke—"

And then I heard it. *DUN! DUN, DUN, DUN!*

as the pounding guitar filled the park. I looked at the crowd and saw Ephie holding her phone high and playing "Eye of the Tiger" as we had told her to do to warn us. I met her sad eyes and saw she was sorry for giving us up.

"It's not only me," I said to Lea and George. "It's *us*. The *three* Spartans. *We* led that team. *We* inspired them."

As I spoke, more kids brought out their cell phones and played "Eye of the Tiger" until it rocked the whole water park.

"This is our triumph. Let's all do the Plunge and show Zeke that *we are Spartans*!"

I held out my fist and Lea put hers on mine. George put his on ours, and together we shouted "Spartans!" and climbed the stairs. All six flights, all the way to the top. From up there I saw, for the first time, the whole of Birch Bay, the town, Terrell Creek—and the forest that hid the treehouse that changed this little town forever. Every kid in the park holding up a cell phone playing our song had been united by our stand at the treehouse.

I bulleted down that slide, taking the Plunge all the way to the bottom. The rush of water around me as I shot out of the tube and into the air was…exhilarating, as my mom would have said.

I slid to the shallow pool and looked behind me. Lea was coming down the slide with George after her. I climbed out of the water and faced Zeke.

He turned red and said, "That doesn't count, anyway. The deal to do the Plunge expired on the weekend. I can still get you kicked out!"

"But you can't get us all kicked out!" one kid yelled and climbed the stairs.

"Which means you can't get any of us kicked out!"

I don't know who said that, but every kid climbed those stairs and took the Plunge. Today, victory belonged to the Spartans. And we were all Spartans!

About the Author

James McCann has written several books for young people, including *Children of Ruin* (Iron Mask Press) and *Flying Feet* (Orca Book Publishers). James teaches creative writing workshops at schools and libraries. When James isn't writing, he's working at Richmond Public Library, playing Dungeons & Dragons or out on a road trip exploring the world. For more information, visit jamesmccann.info.

About Crwth Press

Crwth (pronounced crooth) Press is a small independent publisher based in British Columbia. A crwth is a Welsh stringed instrument that was commonly played in Wales until the mid-1800s, when it was replaced by the violin. We chose this word for the company name because we like the way music brings people together, and we want our press to do the same.

Crwth Press is committed to sustainability and accessibility. This book is printed in Canada on 100 percent post-consumer waste paper using only vegetable-based inks. For more on our sustainability model, visit www.crwth.ca.

To make our books accessible, we use fonts that individuals with dyslexia find easier to read. The font for this book is Helvetica Neue.